"I don't know who you're flying this plane, but if you don't take me back to Kansas City I'll shoot you."

Micah shot a quick glance over his shoulder and fought his surprise. He'd planned for every contingency except the one where a beautiful dark-haired woman in a bridal gown held a gun to his back.

"Who are you?" she demanded. "What are you doing here?"

"I work for an agency that recovers items that haven't been paid for," he replied.

There was a long pause and the "barrel" of the gun bent slightly, letting him know it wasn't a gun at all.

"Oh, my God, I've been rescued by a repo man," she exclaimed, just before he banked the plane slightly to the left.

CARLA CASSIDY

INTERROGATING *the* BRIDE

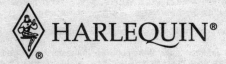

TORONTO • NEW YORK • LONDON
AMSTERDAM • PARIS • SYDNEY • HAMBURG
STOCKHOLM • ATHENS • TOKYO • MILAN • MADRID
PRAGUE • WARSAW • BUDAPEST • AUCKLAND

Recycling programs
for this product may
not exist in your area.

ISBN-13: 978-0-373-69401-3
ISBN-10:   0-373-69401-6

INTERROGATING THE BRIDE

Copyright © 2009 by Carla Bracale

ABOUT THE AUTHOR

Carla Cassidy is an award-winning author who has written more than fifty novels for Silhouette Books. In 1995, she won Best Silhouette Romance from *Romantic Times BOOKreviews* for *Anything for Danny*. In 1998, she also won a Career Achievement Award for Best Innovative Series from *Romantic Times BOOKreviews*.

Carla believes the only thing better than curling up with a good book to read is sitting down at the computer with a good story to write. She's looking forward to writing many more books and bringing hours of pleasure to readers.

Books by Carla Cassidy

HARLEQUIN INTRIGUE

*Cheyenne Nights
†The Recovery Men

Don't miss any of our special offers. Write to us at the following address for information on our newest releases.

Harlequin Reader Service
U.S.: 3010 Walden Ave., P.O. Box 1325, Buffalo, NY 14269
Canadian: P.O. Box 609, Fort Erie, Ont. L2A 5X3

CAST OF CHARACTERS

Caylee Warren—Somebody wants the lovely jewelry store owner dead.

Micah Stone—For the former navy SEAL, a simple mission goes terribly wrong.

Jason Worthington—Had somebody wanted the heir to a fortune dead, or had he simply been at the wrong place at the wrong time?

Grant Worthington—In an effort to save the family name had he done the unspeakable?

Patsy Jackson—Did Caylee's aunt hide a murderous rage beneath her loving smile?

Rick Jackson—He'd been like a brother to Caylee, but had a case of sibling rivalry turned him into a murderer?

Vicki Michaels—How far would the ambitious manager go to have a store of her own?

John Raymond—A local artist. Had his interest in Caylee crossed the line?

Chapter One

In and out, he told himself. That was his job. Get in, get what he was after, then get out before there were any problems.

Micah Stone stood on the deck of the small ferry that would carry him to the tiny island of Fortuna just off the coast of Louisiana. The island, touted as a playground for the rich, was lit like a gaudy Christmas tree rising up from the sea.

This was the last ferry of the night, carrying wealthy tourists from the Louisiana coast to the island that had been transformed by a smart businessman into a semi-private escape for the wealthy and bored. The ferry would begin running again at eight in the morning, but by then Micah would be long gone.

Despite the warm July night air, a faint mist cooled his face and forearms as he leaned on the deck railing and mentally prepared for the job ahead.

As an ex-Navy SEAL he knew all about mentally preparing for an assignment. He drew a deep breath, centered himself and envisioned success. If all went well, within an hour he'd be in a small Cessna 192 plane on his way back to Kansas City.

His partners Troy and Luke would be happy. The bank would be happy. The only unhappy person in the mix would be Jason Worthington, who had managed to get the plane on credit with the power of his family name, and then neglected to make a single payment. The young man refused to take phone calls from the bank about the payments and ignored the letters sent to him.

Loser, Micah thought. It hadn't taken much research to learn that Jason Worthington was a trust-fund brat with few morals and no direction. The bank that had financed the plane had been patient, not wanting to stir the ire of Jason's father, Grant Worthington, a mover and shaker in the Kansas City area. But after almost a year of no payments and no excuses from the young man, the bank had hired Recovery Inc., the business run by Micah and two of his best friends and ex-Navy SEAL buddies.

That morning the men of Recovery Inc. had gotten word that three days ago Jason and his personal pilot had flown from Jason's home in Kansas City to the island of Fortuna for a weeklong visit. The plane now sat on a private runway outside the private residence owned by Jason's grandfather, but if Micah had anything to do with it, the plane wouldn't be there for long.

"Looks like Las Vegas," a female voice said from just behind him. "All the sparkle and glitter out there."

He turned to see a tall, attractive redhead eyeing him with a predator's gaze. He fought a sigh of irritation. He'd come up here on deck to be alone, hoping that nobody would notice him, nobody would be able to identify him if things went bad.

"Yeah," he replied and turned back to face the glittering island, hoping to discourage her from any further conversation.

She sidled up next to him at the railing, engulfing him in the scent of expensive perfume, and placed her hand far too close to his on the railing. A cocktail ring the size of an orange rode one of her fingers. "Staying at one of the hotels?" she asked with a distinctly seductive tone in her voice.

"No," he replied, not giving her any more information.

"I'm staying at The Fountains," she replied, obviously not put off by his disinterest. "My name's Miranda Killory. Just give me a ring if you feel like a party." She smiled and slid her gaze from the top of his head to his feet. "I'm always ready for a party."

Thankfully she drifted away when Micah remained silent. It wasn't the first time an attractive woman had come on to him, but it was definitely one of the most inconvenient.

He breathed a sigh of relief as the ferry approached the dock. He had all that he'd need for the recovery of the plane on his person…his gun and a flashlight. The rest of what he needed was in his head.

He'd memorized the terrain of the island and had plenty of experience in covert operations. He anticipated no trouble as he knew how to get in and out of a situation like a shadow in the night.

Once the ferry had docked, Micah slipped off and disappeared into the thick brush that hugged the bank. According to the maps of the area he'd studied, the Worthington estate was less than three miles away, an easy jaunt for a man in his physical prime.

He took off at a fast pace, the air filled with the noise of the nearby resort and the tangy scent of the sea. Music poured from open doors and the sounds of people rode the faint light breeze.

Micah stayed near the shoreline and moved with the stealth of an animal, creeping forward to where his sources told him the private runway existed at the back of the Worthington estate.

It never failed to amaze him how many wealthy people didn't pay their bills. Recovery Inc. didn't go after the little fellows who got strapped for cash and didn't make a couple of car payments. They were in the big league, repossessing boats and planes and occasionally people who found themselves in trouble.

He shoved all thought of the business aside as he approached the Worthington estate. Despite the fact that it was after midnight, lights shone from the windows of the two-story mansion.

Micah skirted the house and headed for the back where he hoped his sources were right and the Cessna would be sitting on the runway. He didn't expect a guard, but if there was one, Micah knew a dozen ways to incapacitate a man without killing him.

As the runway came into view, a sliver of moonlight danced on the wings of the small plane. Bingo, Micah thought with a sigh of satisfaction.

He crouched down in a stand of brush to one side of the runway and waited. He remained there for just a few minutes to make sure there were no guards, no patrols of any kind for him to encounter.

He never went into an assignment without planning for every contingency. If things went badly he knew not to expect help from any law enforcement agency. At best, the relationship between the men of Recovery Inc. and the local police force was one of strained tolerance. He had a feeling the authorities on Fortuna wouldn't look kindly on him either.

After a few minutes had passed, he was certain that the plane was unguarded, ripe for the picking. Piece of cake, Micah thought as he moved forward.

He'd worn black clothes that would allow him to blend in with the night and he moved across the tarmac at warp speed.

Jason Worthington was so arrogant, so certain he was above the rules that guided ordinary human beings, he not only hadn't posted guards but he also hadn't bothered to secure the plane.

Micah opened the door and climbed into the pilot's seat, pleased that it looked as if he were home free. Within three or so hours of flying, he'd have this little baby back in Kansas City in a hangar owned by Recovery Inc., ready to go back to the bank it now belonged to.

The most dangerous moment would be when he started the engine and prepared for takeoff. If there were guards in the area then the noise of the engine would alert them that something was amiss.

Hopefully he could get in the air before anyone got hurt or an alarm sounded. That was the way these operations were supposed to happen.

It took him only minutes to check that the plane was ready for flight. There was enough gas in the tank to get him back home and he was ready to get out of Dodge.

Troy and Luke would be pleased that the mission went without a hitch and Micah would be home in plenty of time to rest up for his date the next night with a statuesque blonde named Heidi. She was the only woman he knew who wanted a committed relationship less than he did.

He revved up the engines and took off, the euphoric pleasure of flight pulling a smile to his lips. But the smile froze as something poked him in the back, and he felt the warm breath of another person on the nape of his neck.

"I don't know who you are or why you're flying

this plane, but if you don't take me back to Kansas City I'll shoot you."

Micah shot a quick glance over his shoulder and fought his surprise. He'd planned for every contingency except the one in which a beautiful, dark-haired woman in a bridal gown held a gun to his back.

"That's exactly where I'm heading," he replied evenly. "Why don't you put that gun away before it accidentally goes off and somebody gets hurt?"

The pressure in the center of his back didn't move. "Who are you?" she demanded. "What are you doing here? Do you work for Jason?"

"My name isn't important and no, I don't work for Jason."

"Then, what are you doing in his plane?" She had a nice voice, low and melodic. And despite the fact that she held a gun to his back, Micah felt no fear. If her intention had been to shoot him, she would have already pulled the trigger. She wouldn't have waited until they were up in the air. Unless she was a skilled pilot, she wouldn't shoot the man behind the controls.

"I work for an agency that recovers items when they haven't been paid for," he replied.

There was a long pause and the "barrel" of the gun bent slightly, letting him know it wasn't a gun at all. "Oh my God, I've been rescued by a repo man," she exclaimed just before he banked the plane sharply to the left.

CAYLEE WARREN cried out as the plane tilted and she was thrown across the small cabin into the wall on the opposite side.

She fell to the floor and then fought her long, frilly lace dress as she tried to sit up. "What did you do that for?" she complained as she finally righted herself.

"Because I don't like backseat drivers who poke a finger in my back," he replied.

She frowned in dismay. So, he knew it wasn't a gun but rather her finger that she'd used on him. But when he snuck into the plane and prepared to take off and she realized it wasn't Jason's regular pilot, she'd been terrified. It was a state of mind she'd experienced for the past three days.

Once she was on her feet, she scooted into the copilot's seat and looked at the man who, at the moment, controlled her life. "Okay, I don't have a gun," she confessed. "Are you really flying to Kansas City?"

She stared at him. His curly black hair did little to soften his lean, dangerous features and she hoped and prayed she hadn't jumped from a frying pan into a roaring fire.

All she wanted to do was get back to her little apartment in Kansas City. She'd never go off on a trip with a man again unless they were married. In fact, she might never date again, she had so badly misjudged Jason Worthington.

"I'm really flying back to Kansas City," he replied. He turned his head and looked at her for the first time.

His eyes were a startling pale blue and narrowed in cool unfriendliness. "Now you want to tell me who you are and why you were hiding out in the plane? And I'm not even going to ask why you're wearing a wedding gown."

A flush rose to her cheeks. "My name is Caylee Warren. Three days ago I flew down here with Jason to be his guest for a weeklong vacation."

"So how did you get into the back of the plane?"

"I really don't think that's any of your business," she replied. The last thing she wanted was to tell anyone how foolish she'd been. And God, she'd been foolish going off with a man she barely knew.

"Did you marry him or were you playing some kind of fantasy game? You know, doctor and nurse, cheerleader and quarterback, bride and groom."

"Don't be ridiculous," she scoffed, once again a flare of heat warming her cheeks.

"Hey, I'm not the one dressed like a wedding cake topper and hiding in the back of a plane," he replied.

"No, you would be the one stealing a plane," she retorted.

"Not stealing, recovering," he replied. "And if you're going to sit there, buckle in." It was a command rather than a request.

She did as he said, buckling the seatbelt around her. "I told you my name, now why don't you tell me yours."

"Micah Stone."

Micah Stone. She rolled the name around in her head. It suited him. Hard and solid.

It had taken them a little over three hours to fly from Kansas City to the small island of Fortuna, so she was stuck with Mr. Micah Stone for at least the next couple of hours.

She stared out the plane window where the darkness was profound. It was impossible to see landmarks or anything of interest. She couldn't believe she'd gotten herself into such a mess. She'd acted uncharacteristically impulsive with crushing results.

Micah was obviously a man who didn't care much for conversation. The silence stretched between them, thick and uncomfortable, until finally she couldn't stand it any longer.

"This is what you do for a living? Take back things from unsuspecting saps who haven't paid their bills?"

"Jason Worthington isn't exactly an unsuspecting sap," he replied. "He's worth a fortune, but he's not above the law that governs normal people. If you don't pay your bills you lose your toys."

"Jason Worthington is a psychotic creep," she blurted out and then bit her lower lip to stop herself from saying anything more.

Micah cast her a glance that told her he thought it was possible she was one of the toys Jason had bought and paid for. She stiffened her back, deciding she didn't much like Micah Stone.

What she wanted to do was explain the events

that had brought her here, the craziness that had resulted in her hiding in the back of a plane clad in a wedding dress. But Micah Stone deserved no explanation for her behavior.

Once again a tense silence descended between them. She tucked a strand of her long, dark hair behind her ear and cast him a surreptitious look.

He had massive shoulders, and even though he was seated, she could tell his legs were long and lean. Physically he was the type of man who had always made her heart beat just a little faster. But she sensed something dark inside him that told her she didn't want to get to know him any better than what the circumstances warranted.

But she needed something from him, so when he glanced at her with those cool, pale blue eyes, she offered him a friendly smile. "I was wondering if maybe you could do me a favor when we get back to Kansas City?"

"What's that?" he asked, although his tone let her know he didn't particularly like the idea of doing her any favors.

"I don't know where you're dropping off this plane, but would it be possible for you to drive me to my apartment on the north side of town? I don't have my purse with my ID or any money, so taking a cab is out of the question."

"Before I agree to do anything you have to tell me how you ended up in here—dressed like you are—

without your purse or anything else." Those arctic eyes of his gazed at her curiously.

Caylee frowned. She wanted to tell him again that it was really none of his business, but she also needed a ride home. The last thing she wanted to do was call any of her family members and confess her stupidity to them.

"I met Jason about a month ago at the jewelry store I own, Rings and Things. It's in the Oakridge Mall. Ever been there?" It was a stupid question. He didn't look like a man who spent much time in a mall. "Anyway, he seemed charming and bright and when he asked me out, I didn't see any reason not to go. So we'd been seeing each other for the last month, and then he suggested this trip to Fortuna. He told me his family had a place here and that I'd have my own suite of rooms."

She realized she was rambling. She always chattered too much when she was nervous and it suddenly struck her that she had no idea what kind of man Micah Stone was, had no idea if she'd escaped from one psycho into the arms of another.

"Go on," he said curtly.

He didn't look like a psycho. But then Jason hadn't looked like one either, and that man was positively certifiable. She sighed, realizing she really didn't have any other choice but to trust the man in the pilot's seat.

"Anyway, we got there and things were okay, even

though I started noticing things about him that bugged me. By the next day I realized he wasn't anyone I wanted to be with, but I figured I'd finish the trip and once we got back to Kansas City I wouldn't date him anymore. Then tonight he brought me this dress and insisted that I try it on. Then he started talking about how we'd be married as soon as possible and he'd never let me leave his side. That was when I knew I had to get out of there."

She paused a minute, remembering the glint of madness that had shone from Jason's eyes. She'd never been so afraid in her life.

"Anyway, when I went into the bathroom to change out of this dress, I snuck out the window and ran," she continued. "I hid in the plane because I overheard Jason telling his pilot to fly back to Kansas City first thing in the morning and pick up some personal items Jason wanted from his house. I figured I could hide out and be back home before Jason realized I was gone from Fortuna."

She waited for him to say something, to say anything but he remained silent. He probably thought she was all kinds of a fool to go on a weeklong holiday with a man she didn't know well.

"So, are you going to give me a ride home when we get to town or are you going to force me to call one of my relatives and let them know how utterly stupid I've been?" she finally asked.

"I'll drive you home," he said and those were

the last words he spoke to her for the duration of the flight.

Caylee spent the time staring out at the night sky and wondering how she'd been such a bad judge of character. Jason had seemed so nice, so normal during the six dates they'd had before going to Fortuna.

Of course, she'd been out of the dating game for years before she'd met him. Since taking the helm of the jewelry business five years ago, she'd been focused solely on the shop with no time for socializing.

She glanced back at Micah. God, the man was a hunk. Jason had been handsome in a boyish, charming kind of way, but there was nothing boyish about Micah Stone.

The dark clothes he wore only enhanced an aura of hardness, of danger. He looked like a man who could handle anything life threw at him. But just because she liked the way he looked didn't mean she'd like him as a man. In fact, she'd only been in his presence a couple of hours, had only exchanged a few sentences with him, but already she had a feeling that she didn't like him.

But at the moment she needed him. Once he got her safely to her apartment, then she could put him and this entire fiasco behind her.

A sense of relief filled her as the plane descended quickly and she looked down and saw the lights playing on the Missouri River. She assumed he was landing at the downtown airport rather than Kansas

City International Airport, which was to the north of the city. The downtown airport with its shorter runways and close proximity to the river better suited small planes for landing and taking off.

They had just touched down and taxied into a hangar when she heard the distinctive ring of a cell phone. Micah cut the plane engine, reached into his pocket and pulled out the phone.

"Yeah. Just landed and hit the hangar," he said into the phone. He listened for a minute, then cast a narrowed glance toward Caylee. "I picked up a passenger along the way. I'll explain later."

He listened some more, and even though she wouldn't have thought it possible, his features tightened, appeared to grow more lean and dangerous as he stared at her.

"Yes, I understand. Okay. See you in half an hour." He hung up the phone, his gaze still intent on Caylee. "Jason Worthington was found stabbed to death in his family home on Fortuna Island an hour ago. The police are looking for you for questioning." Micah's pale eyes narrowed to slits. "You want to tell me what really happened there tonight or should I just drive you directly to the nearest police station?"

Chapter Two

Micah had to hand it to her, she was either the best actress he'd ever seen or she was genuinely stunned by his words. Her green eyes stared into his as if seeking a punch line to a very bad joke.

"Jason is dead? Murdered?" Her voice was little more than a faint whisper as her face turned as white as the wedding gown she wore. "But that's impossible. He was fine when I left the house."

"That was my partner Luke on the phone. The details coming out of Fortuna are sketchy at the moment, but he thinks it's a good idea if I go underground for a couple of days until we see how this thing shakes down." She stared at him as if he were speaking a foreign language. "Did you kill him?"

His question obviously cut through the fog that had momentarily gripped her. She straightened her back and lifted her chin, her eyes burning overly bright. "I certainly did not." She released a small gasp and shook her head so vehemently her long, dark hair flew around her face. "I just wanted to get away from him. I just wanted to go home. I certainly didn't want him dead."

He unbuckled his seat belt. "We need to get out of here. Luke left his car for me. I'm supposed to meet him and Troy at a safe house our company owns."

He opened the plane door but she grabbed him by the arm, her face still a sickly pallor. "But, what about me? What am I supposed to do?"

Micah had no idea if she was guilty as sin or as innocent as she appeared, but he definitely knew the worst place they could be at the moment was in the plane that had disappeared from Jason Worthington's place on the night he'd been murdered.

"I'm going to meet my partners," he said. "As far as I'm concerned you have two choices," he said, a bit reluctantly. "You can either come with me or I can drop you at your apartment where I imagine you'll be visited by some of the men in blue within the hour."

She frowned, the gesture tugging her dark, perfectly formed eyebrows closer together on her forehead. "I look really guilty," she said more to herself than to him. "I snuck out of a window and ran. Whoever killed him probably did it while I was hiding in the plane, which means I have no alibi." She caught her full bottom lip in her teeth. "I don't know what to do."

"Make up your mind quickly because we need to get out of here," he said tersely.

"Maybe I should come with you until we know more about what happened."

He could tell it was a decision she didn't feel comfortable with, but it obviously beat an arrest for murder. "Then let's do it," he replied.

He left the plane and waited impatiently for her to climb down from the passenger side, the wedding gown hampering her movements. The gown fit her small-framed body perfectly, hugging her slender waist and accentuating the thrust of her breasts against the lacy material. She would have made a beautiful bride.

He had no idea if she was guilty or not. Her story had been far-fetched, but her shock when he'd told her Jason was dead had looked very real.

When she had her feet on the ground they left the hangar and he closed the door and secured the lock before turning to look toward the nearby parking area. His car was there, but he headed toward Luke's sleek sports car, which was parked next to it.

Luke had warned him that it was possible the police would be looking for him, too, and that it might be dangerous for him to be in his own car. How on earth had a simple operation gone so wrong?

As he slid behind the steering wheel, Caylee got into the passenger seat, the gown threatening to engulf her in the narrow seat. Beneath the floor mat he found the keys, just where Luke had said they would be.

He started the engine and pulled out of the parking

lot. Caylee was silent until they were on the highway heading north of the downtown district.

"My apartment is in this direction. I live in the Rockport Apartments. It's a nice place, has a great pool and clubhouse, although I almost never use them because I spend such long hours at the store," she said.

Terrific, not only were things seriously messed up at the moment, he was now trapped in a car with a chatterbox. He cast her a quick glance. She stared out the front window, her pretty features strained as her hands folded and unfolded in her lap.

He could smell the scent of her, a pleasant, slightly exotic fragrance. He hadn't noticed it in the plane but he noticed it now. He gripped the steering wheel more firmly, realizing his hot date with Heidi was probably off.

"This trip with Jason was the first vacation I've taken in five years," she continued. "I can't believe he's dead. Maybe your partner is wrong. Maybe this is all just a terrible mistake." There was more than a little bit of hope in her voice.

"We'll know soon enough," he replied, wishing she'd be quiet for just a minute so he could think. He had a bad feeling in his gut. What should have been a simple mission had suddenly become much more complicated. If Jason Worthington was really dead, then he and Caylee Warren were definitely in trouble.

"Why does your company have a safe house?" she asked.

"Because we occasionally need one." There was no reason for her to know that there were times when Recovery Inc. worked for the government and needed a place to stash a witness or a person in trouble.

He hoped that within the next hour or two she'd go back to her life and he'd go back to his. He had a workout scheduled at the gym in the morning and he wouldn't mind keeping his date with Heidi.

But there was no question that he wasn't feeling good about this whole mess. A lump of uneasiness sat heavy in the pit of his stomach.

He knew without doubt that she was in trouble, but he had a feeling he was deep in the muck as well. He knew there had been surveillance cameras on the ferry and even though he'd tried to stay away from them, he couldn't be sure how successful he'd been.

There was nothing Chief Wendall Kincaid of the Kansas City Police force would like more than to have a reason to arrest Micah. He'd once slept with the chief's sister, but had made the mistake of not proposing marriage. God help him from women who had the Wedding March and a biological clock resounding inside them.

He glanced over at Caylee, who appeared to be growing more nervous with each passing mile. She'd stopped folding and unfolding her hands in her lap and now twisted a strand of her hair around one of her fingers.

She sat up straighter in the seat as he turned off the highway and onto a gravel road lined by tall trees.

They had left the city behind and her nervous tension was palpable in the small car as she cast him furtive glances.

"Don't worry," he said. "I'm not taking you out in the woods to hurt you. The house is an old farmhouse on twenty acres of land."

"That's good because I wouldn't have gone down without a fight." She eyed him with another lift of her chin, then sighed. "I just feel like I've had enough weirdness to last me an entire lifetime."

He didn't know what she was talking about, but he'd certainly categorize finding a bride hiding in the back of a plane right up there on the weird scale.

He released his own sigh as the farmhouse came into view. Majestic oaks flanked the one-story, three-bedroom house, their thick foliage blocking out the moonlight. Lights blazed from the place, and he saw that Troy's car was parked in front.

Good. Both his partners were there. Surely this whole mess could be sorted out in a matter of minutes. He parked next to Troy's car, then doused the lights and unbuckled his seat belt.

Within a couple of hours dawn would break. The long night was beginning to weigh heavy on him. He looked at the woman seated next to him. She really was quite pretty with her heart-shaped face and bright green eyes. But any woman who would buy what Jason Worthington was selling obviously wasn't too bright or was a gold digger with an eye to the Worthington fortune.

As he got out of the car, she fought the ridiculous dress and managed to escape the confines of the car as well. The night air was just as hot, just as humid here as it had been in Louisiana.

"I'm sure this is all just a terrible mistake of some kind," she said again, looking up at him as they headed for the front door.

"We'll know soon enough." He opened the door and ushered her inside. The large living room was decorated like an impersonal hotel suite. The beige sofa was flanked by glass-topped end tables, a coffee table and a matching overstuffed chair set off to one side. An entertainment center held a television, a DVD player and several dog-eared paperback novels.

Caylee followed close behind him, thankfully close-lipped for the moment. He headed for the kitchen where he could hear voices. Troy and Luke would have the most up-to-date news out of Fortuna.

As he entered the kitchen both men stared in his direction. They weren't looking at him but rather over his shoulder to the petite Caylee in her wedding finery.

"Oh man, we're in serious trouble here," Troy said softly, his words tightening the ball of uneasiness in the pit of Micah's stomach.

CAYLEE DIDN'T know what she found more intimidating, being the only woman in the company of men who looked fit enough to take on an entire army all by themselves or the tall blonde's words as he gazed at her.

Micah ushered her into a chair at the table as he made the introductions. Troy Sinclair was an inch or so shorter than Micah who she figured stood at least six foot two. His blond hair was cut short and his eyes were the cool gray of a cloudy day. He was dressed in a crisp, white shirt and a pair of charcoal slacks. A suit jacket hung over the back of his chair.

Luke Washington was about Micah's height with black hair that hung long. He wore a pair of faded jeans and a T-shirt, and looked more biker than businessman. Although both of the other men were attractive, she thought Micah was the most handsome of the three.

She nearly laughed at this thought. She was in trouble. Deep trouble by the sound of things. And yet she was pulling a purely female act by comparing the physical attractiveness of the men she hoped could get her out of this mess.

"What's going on?" Micah asked once all four of them were seated at the table.

"For one thing her picture has been all over the news," Luke said. "Although they're calling her a person of interest, it's pretty clear they think she had something to do with Jason Worthington's murder."

"That's crazy," she exclaimed. "I didn't kill Jason.

All I did was run from him when I got the chance." She felt as if she'd been thrust into a bad dream and couldn't wake up.

"What's equally bad is that they've already tied you to it, too," Troy said to Micah. "Kincaid called my cell an hour ago looking for you. Apparently one of the surveillance cameras on the ferry caught your image and because Jason's permanent residence is here, the locals down there contacted Kincaid. I've got to tell you, it was the first time I've ever heard any real joy in that man's voice."

"Kincaid? Who is that?" Caylee asked.

"Chief of Police. He hates Micah's guts. There's nothing he'd like better than to have a reason, any reason, to lock him up," Troy said.

Caylee looked at Micah, but he offered no further explanation. "Who found the body?" he asked.

"A maid," Luke answered. "Apparently Jason liked a nightcap right before he went to bed and there was a standing order for her to bring him a glass of brandy before he turned in each night. She went to deliver the drink and found him stabbed to death in bed."

All three men turned their attention on Caylee. "I don't know how many ways I can tell you all that I had nothing to do with it." Blood filled her cheeks, warming them in a blush of frustration. "Do any of you see any blood on me? Surely if I'd stabbed Jason I'd be covered in his blood. Or maybe you think I stabbed him, then changed into this wedding gown to make a run for it."

"I meant to ask you about the gown," Luke said.

"Don't ask," Micah replied darkly. "What I want to know is what we should do with her." He thumbed a finger in Caylee's direction as if she were an unsightly wart that had suddenly appeared on the back of his hand.

"Maybe I should just go to the police and tell them I'm innocent," she said. "I mean, surely they would be reasonable."

Micah laughed, a dry bark that held no humor. "The murder took place on Fortuna, which means Louisiana law enforcement will be in charge of the investigation. If you're going to turn yourself in, then be prepared to spend some time there. And you'd better have a great criminal defense lawyer in your corner because right now you look good for this crime."

Each word he spoke filled her more and more with concern. She'd like to believe that no innocent person was ever sent to prison for a crime not committed, but she'd watched enough television to know that simply wasn't the case.

She'd had the means and the opportunity to kill Jason Worthington. More importantly, if she told them that he was acting weird and she'd been frightened of him, then she also had what could be defined as a motive.

"Okay, give me another alternative," she finally said.

"What I recommend is that both of you stay here until we have more information to make some reasonable decisions," Troy said. "The news reports of the murder have been sketchy at best up to this point. It's only been a couple of hours since the body was found, but needless to say because of the Worthington name, things are going to move fast."

Caylee looked at Micah, who returned her gaze with those pale blue eyes that revealed nothing. "Did you meet Jason's father, Grant?"

"No, there was no reason for me to meet him. Jason and I were just casually dating," she replied.

"And you always agree to go off with a man you're casually dating for a weeklong vacation?" Micah asked.

It was obvious by the tone of his voice that he either didn't believe the story she'd told him or he didn't like how she conducted her life. But she didn't care what Micah Stone thought of her or her story. She just wanted this nightmare to end.

"This was my first time to agree to a vacation with a man I was dating. Trust me when I say it will definitely be the last time," she replied.

"Look, I know it's been a long night," Troy said as he got up from the table. "Why don't we all get some sleep. In a couple of hours we'll have more information and we can decide what should be done then."

Luke stood and covered a yawn with the back of his hand. "Why don't we plan on meeting back here around noon?"

Caylee wanted to tell them both to sit back down, to solve this mess right here, right now instead of leaving her alone with Micah, who looked none too happy with the situation.

She remained seated at the table as Micah walked his two partners to the front door. Staring out the window into what was left of the dark night, she thought of the moment she realized she'd needed to escape from Jason.

He'd had her model the wedding gown in his suite of rooms. It had been the last thing she'd wanted to do, but had capitulated in order to keep the peace. After all, Jason was her ride back to the States. As she'd walked into the room his eyes had lit with a fervent light of desire that had pushed her over the edge and made her realize the relationship was going to end badly.

She'd had a feeling that Jason was a man accustomed to getting his own way and it was about to get ugly. She certainly didn't know him or love him enough for a commitment. She hadn't even wanted to sleep with him.

When she'd gone back to her suite of rooms to change, she'd gone directly into her bathroom and it was there she'd decided not to waste another minute. Every internal alarm she possessed was screaming at her to run, to escape. So she'd gone out the bathroom window.

And now he was dead and she was in trouble.

She looked at Micah as he entered the kitchen. "There are three bedrooms. You can pick where you'd like to sleep."

"I don't know if I can sleep," she replied. "I keep going over everything in my mind, trying to figure out what I should have done differently."

"I suggest you try to get some rest. I have a feeling things are only going to get more stressful from here on out."

"I should call my family," she said thoughtfully.

"No phone calls tonight," he said firmly.

She straightened in the chair. "But, they'll be worried about me."

"They'll just have to stay worried for now," he replied. "If it was just you here I wouldn't give a damn who you called, but I'm in this mess, too, and I don't want a slip of your tongue to allow anyone to figure out where we are, so no calls tonight. Now I'll show you the bedrooms." He looked at her expectantly.

She got up from the table. The wedding gown felt as if it weighed a million pounds. "I don't suppose you have a pair of jeans and a T-shirt in my size hanging around."

"No, but I can probably find you a T-shirt and a pair of sweatpants in my size," he replied as they walked through the living room and down a hallway.

"Bathroom is there," he said, pointing to a doorway on the right. She peeked in to see blue towels and a matching shower curtain. "Bedroom one, two and three." He pointed to each of the next three doorways.

She walked into the nearest one where there was a double bed, a dresser and nothing else. "This is fine," she said, suddenly more weary than she'd ever been in her life. She sat on the edge of the bed. "If you could just get me those clothes, I won't bother you anymore."

He nodded and disappeared from the doorway. It hadn't taken her long to realize that Jason was a man who liked to get his own way and she had a feeling Micah Stone was cut from the same cloth. Well, he'd know soon enough that she was a woman who wasn't pushed easily.

He returned with a black T-shirt and a pair of gray jogging pants. He also brought with him a length of rope. "I figured you could use the rope as a belt. I doubt you'll be able to keep those pants up without one. There are new toothbrushes under the sink in the bathroom. Feel free to use anything else in there that you need. I'll see you when you wake up."

He left the room and closed the door behind him. She got up and locked the door, although she had a feeling if Micah wanted to come back inside, no simple lock would keep him out. Still, pressing the button on the doorknob gave her a small sense of control.

Control. She nearly laughed at the idea as she unzipped the hateful gown and stepped out of it. The laughter never materialized, and instead tears burned hot in her eyes.

What a mess. Agreeing to go off with Jason had been uncharacteristic of her, but he'd been charmingly insistent and she'd been too long without both a vacation and a boyfriend.

She pulled on the T-shirt over her bra, instantly engulfed by the fragrance of Micah's faint cologne, a clean scent mixed with a bit of spice. She found it oddly comforting as she pulled down the bedspread and crawled beneath the sheets.

That was her last thought before sleep overtook her. When she woke up, sunshine danced into the nearby window, and by the cast of the sun she figured it must be late morning.

Surely by now the authorities in Fortuna would have caught Jason's killer and her name would be cleared. She could go home, get back to work at the store and put this entire nightmare behind her.

She got out of bed and pulled on the jogging pants, finding them ridiculously big, but certainly better than the damned wedding gown. Using the rope as a belt, she managed to secure them around her waist, then she opened the bedroom door and peered out into the hall.

The scent of coffee rode the air and the sound of voices came from the living room. After listening just a moment she realized the voices were coming from the television.

She went across the hall into the bathroom and stared at her reflection in the mirror above the sink.

The makeup she'd worn the night before hadn't magically disappeared through the long night. Mascara smudged the skin beneath her eyes and gray eye shadow had found the crease in her eyelids and clung heavily.

She eyed the shower longingly and gave into temptation. She'd face the day better if she could wash the night off her. She stood beneath a hot spray of water and wished the events of the night before had been nothing more than a crazy nightmare. She wanted to step out of the shower and be back in her apartment, getting ready for a day at the store.

But of course that didn't happen. She redressed in the sweats and T-shirt, brushed her teeth with one of the new toothbrushes and worked the tangles out of her hair. Finally she felt prepared to take on whatever the day might bring.

Vindication, that's all she wanted— That and a return to her normal, boring life. It was going to be a long time before she'd be interested in an exotic vacation again.

Micah sat on the sofa, looking more stern, more dangerous than he had the night before. A weight of dread filled her stomach. He didn't look like a man pleased with the morning news.

"Good morning," she said.

His head moved in a curt nod. "Coffee is in the kitchen and there are some doughnuts as well."

"What's happened since last night?" she asked.

"Go get your coffee and then we'll talk," he replied. His eyes gave nothing away, but she knew the news wasn't good.

In the kitchen she found the coffee pot half full and a box of glazed doughnuts on the table. She poured herself a cup of coffee but ignored the doughnuts. Her stomach was twisted in too many knots to eat.

With coffee cup in hand, she returned to the living room and sat on the opposite end of the sofa from Micah. Once again she was struck by his handsomeness. He wasn't a pretty boy—his features were too bold, too lean to be considered handsome in the classic sense.

She ignored the slight flutter in her stomach just as she'd ignored the doughnuts. The last thing she needed at the moment was to feel any kind of attraction for another man. It was a man who'd gotten her into this debacle.

"Unfortunately things look less promising for us this morning than they did last night," he said as he pressed a remote control button that muted the television.

She glanced at the screen where an attractive blonde stood in front of a weather map, then looked back at Micah, dreading whatever he was about to tell her.

"What do you know about the maid who was in Fortuna with you and Jason," he asked.

She sat back and frowned. "Not much. Her name is Marie. She's about my age, maybe a little older. I got the impression she's worked for the Worthington family for years. Why?"

"She's been all over the news, telling every reporter who will listen that she knew you were nothing more than a gold digger when she met you, and that she knows you killed poor young Mr. Worthington, then stole valuables from the house."

Caylee gasped. "But that's crazy. I didn't steal anything from there except the gown that I wore out. As far as me being a gold digger, that's utterly ridiculous. I have my own money. I didn't need any from Jason Worthington. My jewelry store was financially successful when my father owned it, and when he died five years ago and it passed to me, I managed to increase profits tenfold. I'm a wealthy woman in my own right." She stopped her tirade to draw breath. "If anything was stolen last night then I would suggest they check the maid's luggage."

"The general consensus seems to be that you and I were in this together." His pale eyes bore into hers with a hint of acrimony. "The theory is that you killed Jason and stole a bunch of stuff and I was there as the getaway driver, so to speak."

"This is all crazy. How can this be happening," she said more to herself than to him.

"The how doesn't matter," he replied, his voice terse. "What does matter is that as of ten o'clock this morning, arrest warrants were issued for both of us."

Once again Caylee released a gasp. She grabbed

hold of the sofa's arm, feeling as if the world had suddenly tilted and she was about to fall off. "I don't understand, how could they have done that already? What happened to an investigation?"

"It's called a rush to judgment," he said. His gaze left hers and focused on the television where the words, "Murder in Paradise" danced across the bottom of the screen. He hit the remote button to bring up the sound to hear a male reporter speaking.

"…Marie Carvel made a grisly discovery. Curled in a fetal ball beneath the gold and pink bedspread was the body of her employer. Jason Worthington had been stabbed three times with a knife that has yet to be recovered."

Caylee shot up rigid, her heart pounding in stunned surprise. "Mute it," she exclaimed.

"What's wrong?" Micah asked, hitting the mute button.

She stared at him. "The gold and pink bedspread they just talked about, that wasn't in Jason's room. The bedspread in his room was navy. The pink and gold, that was the bedspread in my room." She frowned. "While I was in the bathroom escaping out the window, Jason must have come into my room and gotten into my bed."

"Wouldn't the killer have seen his face?"

Caylee frowned. "Not necessarily. Maybe he had the blanket up over his head. He was childish like that."

Micah stared at her for a long minute. "So, that

means one of two things," he said slowly. "The killer had to have followed him from his room to your room."

"You said two things," she said, her heart began to beat in an unsteady rhythm as she anticipated his next words.

"Or Jason wasn't the intended victim at all," he said, his words causing an arctic chill to crawl up her back.

"You were."

Chapter Three

Micah watched as Caylee jumped up from the sofa and began to pace back and forth in front of him. He couldn't help but notice how attractive she looked this morning with her freshly scrubbed face and her shiny dark hair.

He found it more than a little irritating that despite the fact that she wore a T-shirt that was far too big and jogging pants that engulfed her, the thrust of her full breasts was evident as was the sexy sway of her hips.

"Who would want to kill me?" she said, her voice almost a full octave higher than normal. "I don't have any enemies, I try to be nice to everyone I meet. I'm a thoughtful employer, I don't owe anybody money and I don't have any crazy ex-boyfriends." She stopped pacing and stared at Micah. "Why would anyone want me dead?"

"Maybe because you talk so much?" he said dryly.

Her cheeks colored with a blush and she shot him a cool frown. "I always talk too much when I'm nervous," she said. "And excuse me, but the possibility that somebody tried to kill me definitely makes me more than a little bit nervous."

"Why don't you sit down. You're starting to make *me* nervous," Micah said gruffly. He was irritable this morning. He'd gotten little sleep the night before and the news of the day certainly hadn't made him feel better about the mess he'd stepped into when he'd gotten on that plane in Fortuna.

He frowned as Caylee flopped down next to him. "So, what are we going to do?" she asked, her glittering green eyes looking at him questioningly. "Maybe we should just turn ourselves in, explain to the police what happened and that we didn't have anything to do with Jason's death. Surely we can make them see that we're innocent."

"You're free to do that if you want. Unfortunately it's not the path I intend to follow. There's a bit of bad blood between me and Chief Kincaid. If I turn myself in, he'll make sure I don't see the light of day for a long time to come," Micah said.

He could see the questions in her eyes, questions he didn't intend to answer, so he continued. "However if you do choose to turn yourself in, let me remind you of what I said last night—I hope you have somebody good to run your shop and plenty of money to hire a high-powered criminal defense lawyer. A murder trial steals time and money from everyone involved except the lawyers."

She should never play poker, he thought as he watched the myriad expressions that played on her features. Shock, disbelief and fear, they were all there in her eyes, on her face.

"I can't leave my store indefinitely with my manager in charge of things," she said. "I mean, she's a nice young woman, but I need to be there making the decisions and keeping things running smoothly. I haven't spent the last five years of my life working my butt off to make it a success for it all to go to ruin because of this…this mistake."

She leaned toward him and placed a hand on his forearm, the icy cold of her fingers telling him she wasn't as composed as she was trying to appear. "So, what are we going to do?" she asked again.

Micah shifted positions, dislodging her hand from him. He didn't want her looking to him for answers. He'd spent his entire life consciously choosing not to be responsible for anyone but himself. He definitely didn't want to be responsible for a woman he didn't know, a woman at the center of a murder case. He had enough problems of his own.

And yet, what was he supposed to do? Throw her out of the house? Leave her to flounder on her own because her eyes were too green, her face was too pretty and her very presence made him slightly uncomfortable?

"Micah?" She held his gaze intently, looking as if she were waiting for him to fix her world.

Before he could formulate an answer, the front door opened and Troy and Luke came in. They carried in their arms several bags of groceries and wore the same grim expressions they'd had the night before.

Both Caylee and Micah followed them into the kitchen where they began to unload the food and put it away. "It doesn't look like this is all going to resolve itself easily. There's talk that the officials on Fortuna are going to give the investigation into Jason's death to the Kansas City cops," Troy said as he shoved a couple packages of steaks into the freezer.

"Why would they do that? The murder took place in their jurisdiction." Micah sat at the table across from Caylee.

"Officially the reasoning is Jason wasn't a resident at the time of his death and they're certain that the people who committed the crime, you and Caylee, have returned to Kansas City," Troy replied.

"Unofficially, it's probably because the Fortuna police force is a handful of glorified security guards," Luke added. "Murder wasn't supposed to happen on the glittering island on the sea."

"Besides, by handing it over to the Kansas City cops they manage to distance the island from the murder. The last thing the officials on Fortuna want is for the island to be in the news as a place where the rich and infamous might not be safe." Troy put the last of the meat they'd brought into the refrigerator, then joined them at the table.

"So, what does that mean for us?" Caylee asked.

"It means every cop on the Kansas City police force will be looking for you two." Luke flung himself into the last chair at the table, his dark eyes glittering.

"We discovered something interesting when watching the news," Micah said. He told them about Jason being murdered in the bed where Caylee had been sleeping. "We think it's possible Jason wasn't the intended victim."

Both Luke and Troy focused their attention on Caylee, whose cheeks blossomed pink beneath their intense scrutiny. "I can't imagine who'd want to hurt me," she said.

Micah leaned back in his chair. "But we have to consider the possibility that she was the target, not Jason." He looked at Caylee once again. "And that means I'm going to get very well acquainted with you and your lifestyle." His tone of voice was harsh, making it sound more like a threat than he'd intended. So much for staying uninvolved, he thought to himself. "The only way to clear my name is to clear yours."

His interest in her was purely self-serving. At the moment he needed her because she was the answer to getting himself out of this mess.

"I'll do whatever you tell me to," she said as she sat up straighter in the chair. "I just don't know where to begin. This is all new to me, being accused of murder and staying with three repo men."

"Recovery experts," Micah corrected her.

"Whatever," she exclaimed.

"It looks like the only way to get you out of trouble is to solve the crime ourselves." Troy raked a hand over his short blond hair, a gesture Micah knew indicated a certain level of stress.

Troy and Luke had become the family Micah had never had, brothers of the heart bonded by the experience of war, mutual respect and that indefinable element that forges lifelong friendships.

He knew he was putting them at risk as accessories to murder. They could face charges of aiding and abetting. But he also knew not to protest their involvement, knew that they would have his back whether he wanted them to or not.

"We'll spend the day digging up what we can on Jason Worthington," Luke said. His dark eyes glittered with the thrill of the chase. "By the end of the day we'll not only know who his friends and enemies were, we'll also know what he had for breakfast the day he died and what his favorite color was."

"I can tell you what he had for breakfast," Caylee said. "Marie served us fruit cups and croissants. We didn't want to eat anything too heavy because he'd planned on us spending the day on the beach. I'm not a huge beach person, but I was eager to get out of the house and spend the day among other people because Jason was giving me the willies."

Troy and Luke looked at her as if she were a creature from another planet. "She talks too much when she gets nervous," Micah explained dryly.

"I'd plan on the two of you being here for at least a week or longer," Troy said, once again looking at Micah. "You know investigating anything like this takes time."

"Is there any way I can go to my apartment and get some clothes and things?" Caylee asked. She grabbed the bottom of the T-shirt she wore.

"You can't," Troy replied. "I'm sure the cops are probably watching the place."

"I can get in and get you what you need," Luke said.

"Really?" The smile that curved her lips tightened a ball of tension inside Micah's stomach. Her smile immediately disappeared. "I don't have my keys," she said with obvious dismay. "Surely it would be easier just to pick up a few things from the store."

"I'd rather break in someplace than shop for a woman," Luke replied.

"Luke doesn't need keys," Micah replied. One of Luke's strengths was that he'd never met a lock he couldn't pick or an alarm system he couldn't disarm. "He'll be fine."

"I'll get in tonight after dark. Just make a list of things you want from there," Luke said.

Micah got up and moved to a cabinet drawer where he pulled out a legal pad and a pen. He gave them both to Caylee, but remained standing, knowing instinctively that within minutes Luke and Troy would be leaving.

Troy scooted his chair back. "So, we're all on the same page?"

Micah nodded as Caylee hurriedly wrote out her list for Luke. When she was finished she handed the sheet of paper to him and together Luke and Troy stood.

Micah walked with them to the front door, surprised to realize he was dreading the moment they'd walk out and leave him alone with Caylee.

"Anything you need us to take care of for you?" Troy asked as they paused just inside the door. He grinned. "I mean other than the obvious."

Micah had no family to contact, nobody who would care if he disappeared off the face of the earth forever. Even Heidi, the tall blonde he was supposed to meet tonight, would quickly find another man to fulfill her basic needs. The only people who might notice his absence were his neighbors, and then only to bitch and moan about the fact that he wasn't keeping up with his lawn.

"Let's just get to the bottom of this as fast as we can so I can get back to my life," Micah finally said.

"We'll also see what we can dig up on the maid, Marie Carvel. She's doing a lot of mouth flapping to reporters," Troy added.

"I'll be by late tonight with Caylee's things," Luke said and with that, Micah's two partners left the house. "You have spare clothes, right?" he said to Micah, who nodded.

Micah watched them as they got into a car he'd never seen before. They were being careful, aware that Chief Kincaid would be watching them. Micah tightened his grip on the door as he closed it. Kincaid would probably love to have an opportunity to put a bullet through Micah's heart.

He also noticed dark storm clouds gathering in the southwest, portending rain in the near future. Micah hated rain. Everything bad that had ever happened in his life had happened during a storm.

He returned to the kitchen where Caylee had poured herself a fresh cup of coffee and had indulged in one of the doughnuts. Her upper lip was dusted with a fine coat of sugar and for just one moment of temporary insanity, Micah wanted to lean across the table and lick it off.

"What do we do now?" she asked.

He grabbed a napkin from the holder in the center of the table and thrust it at her with more force than necessary. Her eyes widened as she quickly ran it across her full lips.

"What happens next is that I learn everything there is to know about you and your life, and we try to figure out who might want you dead."

It had been a long time since he'd been so acutely conscious of a woman. Even now he was aware of the scent of her, the clean, fresh fragrance of the soap they kept in the bathroom. The smattering of freckles across her nose was now evident without the cover of her makeup, but rather than making her look young and vulnerable, the freckles looked oddly sexy.

At that moment a boom of thunder shook the windows, and the ball of dread that had been inside Micah's belly since the moment they'd heard about Jason's murder tightened into a hot pool of fire as he fully realized the danger of the storm around them.

"I HATE STORMS," Caylee said as she looked out the window where the sunny sky had been usurped by dark, angry clouds. "Especially summer storms." She looked back at Micah, her eyes darker green than they'd been a moment ago. "When I was eight years old, my mother died of cancer. The night she finally passed there was a terrible storm. My dad came out of the hospital room and told me she was gone. For a long time afterward I thought the storm had taken her away."

Micah reached in front of her and pulled the legal pad and pen in front of him. "So, your father raised you?"

She smiled. "My father loved me, but for all intents and purposes, he didn't really raise me, my Aunt Patsy took care of me."

"What's Patsy's legal name?" He picked up the pen and she noticed that his hands were big and looked strong. There wasn't a single part of the man that seemed soft or vulnerable.

"Surely you don't think my Aunt Patsy has anything to do with this," she protested. She couldn't imagine the plump, loving woman who'd taken her and her cousin to play in the park, the woman who had gone shopping for Caylee's first bra and had taught her the facts of life, being in any way responsible for the murder.

Another rumble of thunder sounded, and Caylee jumped in her chair. Rain began to pelt the windows and she wasn't sure if it was the storm that stirred the darkness inside her or the very idea that somebody close to her might want to kill her.

"This has got to be about Jason," she said fervently. "His killer must have followed him from his suite to mine. I just can't imagine this has anything to do with me. I was just at the wrong place at the wrong time." She desperately wanted him to agree with her, to tell her that everything was going to be all right.

Unfortunately platitudes didn't appear to be a part of Micah Stone. "What's Patsy's last name," he repeated.

"Jackson, Patricia Jackson," she said and wished her Aunt Patsy was with her right now, and could wrap Caylee up in her plump, loving arms.

"Any other family?"

"Just my cousin, Rick. He's twenty-eight, two years younger than me. We were raised more like brother and sister than cousins."

"What does he do?"

"He's a computer and electronics geek and runs a repair shop out of his house." She sighed with frustration. "Look, there's no way these people would hurt me. They're my family. We love each other. We've never exchanged a cross word between us."

"I'm just getting background information," he said, his voice emotionless and his pale eyes making her want to scream.

"Why don't you tell me a little of your background," she said. "For the moment it looks like we're stuck here together, it would be nice if I knew something about you."

For just a moment a touch of humor shone from his eyes. "All you need to know about me is that I'll never take you to an island, buy you a wedding dress and force you to run and hide in the back of a plane."

"Very funny," she exclaimed. She knew from his answer that he had no intention of telling her anything meaningful about himself.

"This isn't about me," he continued. "I was just there to recover a plane. This is about you and Jason Worthington. Troy and Luke are picking apart his life, and it's my job to pick apart yours."

She twisted the napkin between her fingers. She wanted to be angry with Micah for not being reassuring or sympathetic, for not taking her into his arms and holding her until the chill inside her warmed.

But she supposed if he was going to find the killer it was better that he was single-minded, objective and on her side. Of course she couldn't forget that he was on her side for one reason only. Until he cleared her name, his wouldn't be cleared either.

"What else do you want to know?" she finally asked, resigned that she had to get through this line of questioning.

"You mentioned that you hadn't been dating, that Jason was your first boyfriend in a long time." This time his facial expression was one of disbelief. "A pretty woman like you surely had men interested in a relationship with you."

A feminine flutter of pleasure swept through her. He thought she was pretty. The flutter lasted only a moment, then halted as she reminded herself she didn't care what Micah Stone thought of her. He was merely the means to an end.

"Like I told you before, I've focused solely on work the last five years. There hasn't been time for romance or men." She twisted the napkin around her ring finger. "I'm not one of those women who needs a man in my life to feel complete. A relationship would be a wonderful addition to my life, but it's not a necessity." She winced, recognizing she'd given him more information than he'd asked for. "Anyway, the answer is no, there are no crazy boyfriends lurking in my past."

She got up from the table and grabbed another one of the doughnuts in the box. Sugar. Maybe a taste of sugar would ease the edge of despair that threatened to consume her.

"What about coworkers?" Micah asked, watching her with slightly narrowed eyes as she returned to the table, the doughnut in hand. "Have you fired anyone recently?"

"No, most of the people who work for me have been with me for years." She frowned thoughtfully. "But I did recently hire a new guy. He's only been working at the store for a month."

"Name?"

"Marvin. Marvin Bishop. He had a good work history."

"What about a criminal background? Do you check your employees for that kind of thing?"

"No. All the people I've hired have come to me with references from people in the jewelry industry that I know."

"Has he shown an unusual interest in you? Made any kind of inappropriate comments or actions?"

Caylee leaned back in her chair and dropped the napkin she'd begun to methodically shred. "If he had, he wouldn't be working for me any longer."

The morning changed into afternoon with question after question from Micah. He took notes on the legal pad as rain continued to beat against the windows.

It was after three when she finally called a halt. She was stiff from sitting in the kitchen chair, hungry for something more than doughnuts and coffee, and tired of feeling as if her life was under the microscope of Micah's sharp, intense eyes.

"I'm done," she announced, "and if I don't get some real food, I'm going to get real cranky."

"We don't want that," Micah said, shoving away the legal pad and standing up. He stretched with his arms overhead and his dark T-shirt rode up slightly to expose a six-pack of taut, tanned abdomen. No matter what the reasons, as her gaze slid up to his big shoulders and broad chest, she was glad this man was on her side and not against her.

"What sounds good?" he asked as he lowered his arms and walked over to the refrigerator.

"Anything," she replied. "As long as the basic component isn't sugar."

"How about I broil a couple of steaks, and while I'm doing that you can make us a salad."

"Sounds like a plan," she agreed, eager to do anything that involved some sort of activity besides sitting and thinking about the people close to her.

He pulled steaks from the refrigerator and as he seasoned them and put them on the broiler pan, she got out the ingredients for the salad.

It didn't take long for her to realize the kitchen suddenly seemed too small for the both of them. Micah was so big, so capable-looking. She had no doubt that if a criminal burst through the front door, Micah would take him out as easily as if he were taking out the garbage.

As she tore lettuce and chopped up tomatoes and peppers, she wondered what he'd look like if he smiled. She wondered what his laughter would sound like.

Then she wondered why she was wondering. It wasn't as if she and Micah were here together by choice. Although he was definitely a major hunk, personality-wise he wasn't the kind of man who usually drew her in. She liked men who smiled not only with their mouths but also with their eyes. She liked charming and charismatic men.

She frowned and chopped the green pepper faster. Jason had been charismatic, with a smile that would have lit the night sky. And look what happened with him. Maybe quiet and aloof was a better choice for the future.

"Are you killing that pepper or cutting it?" Micah asked, pulling her from her thoughts. She realized that thinking about Jason had put more force in her knife than necessary.

"A little of both," she admitted. She set the knife aside, leaned against the counter and cast her glance outside. The rain had stopped, but the sky was a somber gray. A perfect reflection of the mood that was slowly taking over her.

She looked back at Micah. "It's rather distressing to spend the day wondering if somebody you know, somebody close to you, tried to kill you. Every person we spoke about today is somebody I care about, somebody who I thought cared about me."

For just a moment she thought she saw a softening in his eyes and she wanted to take advantage of it. "Talk to me, Micah. Talk to me about anything but murder and suspicion."

He shrugged uneasily. "I'm really not much of a talker."

"We both know that I am, and if you don't talk to me then I'll talk to you," she warned with a smile.

"Then maybe I better figure out something to talk about." He smiled then, and it was like a gift of warmth. The gesture humanized his stern features and those cold, blue eyes of his sparked to life.

Her breath caught in her chest and for a sweet instant, she forgot what had brought her here, forgot the threat that hung over their heads.

What she wanted to do more than anything was make him smile once again, but instead he turned around to the oven and opened the door to check on the steaks.

"So, tell me how you met Troy and Luke," she said a few minutes later as they sat down to eat.

"Basic training."

"Army?"

He shook his head. "Navy. Actually we were all SEALS."

That explained the buff bods, the air of competence and her almost immediate feeling that she was in good hands.

"We first got close when we realized we were all from Kansas City, then time and experience did the rest. They're the brothers I never had. I'd trust them with my life."

She glanced out the window where the storm had created an early false twilight. "Do you think Luke will be all right trying to get into my apartment? I mean, if the police are watching it, how's he going to get in without being seen?"

"Don't worry about Luke. He's like a shadow in the night. Nobody will see him get in or get out. That's his particular skill."

"And Troy? Does he have a special skill?"

Again a glimmer of a smile shone from his eyes. "Troy is our front man. He comes from money, is as smooth as silk in getting into places where Luke and I wouldn't know which spoon to use."

"And you?" she asked.

The glimmer in his eyes became a wicked gleam. "I like speed. Fast cars, planes, boats and women." The last word was said with emphasis, as if he were warning her, as if he knew she wasn't a fast woman and would do well to keep her distance from him. She'd be glad to—as soon as they solved the mystery of Jason's murder.

The rest of the dinner conversation was the kind of inane talk that strangers share. They spoke of the growth of the city, the new mayor and the unusually stormy summer.

What she really wanted to know was where he came from, who he was beneath the cool eyes and broad shoulders. She wondered if her interest in him was simply because she didn't want to think about the bigger, more pressing issues facing her.

After dinner they turned on the television, channel surfing for any of the latest news concerning the murder on Fortuna, but the information was the same as it had been that morning.

An uncomfortable silence built between them as the evening deepened and they waited for Luke to appear. It was an odd feeling for Caylee, to worry about a man she barely knew. But she knew whatever chances Luke was taking were for her, and she'd feel forever responsible if anything went wrong.

"Stop worrying," Micah said softly.

She flashed him a quick smile and changed positions, burrowing deeper into the corner of the overstuffed sofa. "I can't help it. And worrying about Luke makes me think about my Aunt Patsy and how worried she probably is right now about me."

A frown raced across Micah's forehead. "We'll see if we can figure out a way to contact her and let her know you're okay."

"Thanks, I'd really appreciate it. Aunt Patsy and my cousin Rick are all the family I have left since my dad died." She focused back on the television where troubles in Iraq were the topic of the hour.

She must have dozed off because the sound of the front door opening awakened her, and she sat up as Luke came in carrying a large black bag.

"Any trouble?" Micah asked.

"None." Luke dropped the bag on the floor. "The police must not think there's too much of a chance she'll show up at her apartment. There was only one patrol car babysitting the building."

"Thank you so much," Caylee said. "I know I'll feel better if I can get into my own clothes."

"Yeah, well, I have a little item I picked up in your apartment that isn't going to make you feel so good," Luke replied. He bent over and unzipped the bag, his long hair momentarily obscuring his features. "Thank God I got inside before the cops decided to get a warrant and search your place."

He withdrew a plastic storage bag and laid it on the coffee table. Caylee stared at the item contained within the bag, a growing sense of horror sweeping through her.

Inside the bag was a butcher knife...a bloody butcher knife.

Chapter Four

Micah watched as Caylee rose from the sofa, her slender hand trembling as it swept up to tuck a strand of hair behind her ear. "I don't understand. What is that?" She stared at the knife as if she'd never seen one before. Micah got up from his chair and looked at the knife for an agonizing moment, his stomach filling with a heavy rock of dread.

"I'd say what we have here is a murder weapon," Luke replied. He looked at Caylee, then at Micah. "The authorities didn't find it at the crime scene in Fortuna. I'd guess that when it wasn't you beneath the sheets on that bed, our killer shifted to plan B."

"Plan B?" Caylee's voice was faint and her beautiful eyes shone overly bright as she looked first at Luke, then at Micah.

"He was unsuccessful in killing you, so the next best thing is to plant the murder weapon in your apartment and put you in prison for the rest of your life," Micah said. "Somebody wants you out of commission permanently, one way or another."

The mist in her eyes grew more pronounced. "Who is doing this?" she asked. "Who would hate me enough to do something like this?" Tears spilled onto her cheeks, and without warning she launched herself at Micah.

She burrowed against his chest like a baby robin seeking shelter from a storm in the warmth of mother's feathers.

Helplessly, he looked over her head to Luke, who suddenly seemed far too intent on refastening the zipper on the duffel bag.

The scent of her clean hair filled Micah's nose and the warm curves that pressed against him stirred him on an unwanted level. He kept his arms at his sides. There was a part of him that wanted to push her away, a part that needed to distance himself from the startling physical reaction she evoked in him.

She raised her head and looked up at him, her green eyes awash with tears. "Hold me, Micah," she said, her voice holding a faint demand. "Please, I need you to wrap me in your arms and hold me tight."

The plea came from her heart, and as she laid her head back against his chest there was no question that he would do as she'd asked.

Tentatively he raised his arms and embraced her as she began to weep once again. He tried to imagine what it must be like, to have to face the fact that somebody you trusted, perhaps somebody you loved, wanted you dead or in prison.

Micah had known from an early age not to trust or depend on anyone, but he had a feeling for a woman like Caylee, the situation would be devastating.

She finally stopped crying and once again looked up at him. "Promise me this is going to be all right." Her eyes gleamed with the need of something, anything to hang on to.

His stomach clenched. He wanted to give her what she wanted, what she needed, but he couldn't. "I don't believe in promises," he said truthfully. "But, I can tell you that we're going to do everything in our power to make things right."

She frowned, her gaze turning curious. He dropped his arms from around her and took a step back, directing his gaze at Luke. "I'd like you to get a couple of prepaid throwaway phones."

Luke nodded. "Anything else?"

"Just information, although I think we can safely say now that the intended victim in this is Caylee." He stared at the knife in the bag on the table.

"We did have a chat this afternoon with one of Jason's friends. He told us Grant Worthington was putting pressure on his son to settle down, that he'd threatened Jason with disinheritance." Luke moved closer to the front door as Caylee returned to her seat in the corner of the sofa. She wrapped her arms around herself as if seeking to banish a chill that had her in its grip.

"Apparently he had a woman all picked out for Jason, a wealthy debutante. Old family money, a merging of fortunes." Luke shrugged. "Maybe Daddy didn't like his son dating a shopkeeper."

"Surely you can't believe that a man like Grant Worthington would try to kill the woman his son was dating," Caylee exclaimed.

"Who knows? The wealthy, they function with a different set of rules than the rest of us," Luke said.

Micah smiled. "Don't let Troy hear you say that."

Luke flashed one of his quicksilver grins. "Troy is the exception, not the rule, when it comes to the wealthy. He actually has a heart, a soul."

"Couldn't it be possible that somebody Jason dated in the past might not have wanted me in his life?" Caylee asked, obviously still wanting to make the guilty party be somebody she didn't know, somebody she didn't trust. "An old girlfriend hoping to marry into the Worthington money might have seen me as a threat."

"At this point anything is possible," Micah said, pleased that her tears had dried and her gaze was once again focused and clear. He raked a hand through his hair, suddenly too tired to think.

"I'm out of here," Luke said, as if reading Micah's thoughts. "It's late. I recommend you both get a good night's sleep and we all start fresh in the morning."

Caylee once again rose from the sofa. "Thank you, Luke, for getting my things." She smiled at him and Micah wished that smile was directed his way. But that ridiculous thought filled him with a vague irritation.

"Not a problem. We'll check in sometime tomorrow and I'll get those phones to you." Without another word, he slid out of the door and disappeared into the darkness of the night.

Micah walked to the door and locked it as Caylee picked up the duffel bag from the floor. "I'm just going to take this to my room and unpack it," she said.

He nodded, eager to gain a little distance from her. He couldn't stop thinking about how she'd felt in his arms, so soft and so tiny. "If you need me for anything I'm in the back bedroom," he said as he followed her down the hallway.

A flash of lightning lit the hallway, announcing the wave of new storms that the weatherman had predicted would affect the area throughout the night. A distant rumble of thunder followed the lightning.

He murmured a good-night to Caylee as she went into her bedroom, then continued down the hall to his own. His was the master suite and not only contained a king-size bed and dresser, but also a desk with a computer. They rarely used this house, but when they had been setting it up, they'd decided that both a computer and satellite television were necessities, each of them tools for keeping in touch with the outside world.

Once in the bedroom, he pulled his gun from his ankle holster and set it on the nightstand. He then shucked his jeans and pulled his T-shirt over his head. Clad only in his briefs, he got into bed. He was exhausted but he knew that sleep wouldn't come easy. It never did when there were storms.

He closed his eyes and tried not to wonder what kind of nightwear Caylee wore. Was she the type to wear cotton pajamas or a silk nightgown? Did she prefer a T-shirt and panties or did she sleep naked?

If he were to be perfectly honest with himself, he'd have to acknowledge that it wasn't just the fact that she had sexy hips and full breasts that reluctantly attracted him.

She'd impressed him with her strength. Other than the brief crying jag when she'd seen the knife that had been left in her apartment, she'd held up remarkably well given the circumstances.

He believed her when she said she hadn't been hurtful to anyone, that she couldn't imagine who might be doing this to her. There was a softness about her, a light that shone from her eyes that was filled with kindness. And yet she'd been strong enough not to fall to pieces, strong enough to ask for what she wanted.

He thought of her telling him she needed him to put his arms around her and hold her. He liked that she spoke of her need, instead of waiting for him to somehow figure it out.

With a sigh of irritation, he turned and punched

the pillow beneath him, then flopped back down, staring up at the darkened ceiling.

What he should be thinking about was how to get them out of this mess and out of this house. He closed his eyes against another flash of lightning that split the darkness of the room.

A wave of unexpected loneliness swept through him. He consciously willed it away as he had all his life. Experience had taught him that he could only depend on himself, that life was just a series of storms to be survived and as far as he was concerned, Caylee Warren was just another storm.

"TELL ME AGAIN, who has keys to your apartment?" Micah's voice possessed the hard edge that it had held all morning. It was almost noon, and they had been at it since nine, him hammering her with question after question about her life.

"I've already told you," she protested, nerves chattering inside her like demented castanets.

"Tell me again," he demanded.

He'd been distant and demanding since the moment she'd gotten up. The night had seemed endless, with not just the thunder and lightning keeping her awake but also the very questions he'd been asking her since she'd stumbled into the kitchen for her first cup of coffee.

Who and why? Those were the two words that had kept her tossing and turning until near dawn. Who would want to do this to her and why?

She leaned back, wondering which felt harder, the wooden rungs of the chair behind her or the intensity of Micah's gaze.

"My Aunt Patsy has a key. So does my neighbor, Samantha, and my store manager, Vicki. But none of those people could possibly be involved in any of this. None of them left that knife in my apartment."

"Why not?"

"Because these are people who care about me." She felt like she'd been saying this over and over again, and he just wasn't hearing her.

"Are you absolutely sure? Or are they people who pretend to care about you? Sometimes people can smile in your face while they're stabbing you in the back."

She frowned at him, noting how the sunlight drifting in though the windows played on his chiseled, strong features. "What kind of a world do you come from where that's what happens?"

He blinked and looked away, and for the first time she noticed the length and thickness of his eyelashes. God, the man was such a hunk…and such a mystery.

"The real world," he replied.

"That's not my world. I think it's tragic if that's yours," she replied. What kind of a life did he have that friends and relatives could be suspects in heinous crimes?

Before he could reply, a knock sounded on the front door. In the blink of her eye, a gun filled

Micah's hand and he was up from the table. "Stay here," he commanded.

As he left the kitchen, Caylee couldn't have moved if a bomb went off beneath her. Even though she'd known they were in trouble with the law, she hadn't really considered that a threat of real, physical danger existed until she'd seen his gun.

He returned a moment later, followed by Troy. "Sorry, I forgot my key," Troy said. He carried with him a shopping bag and set it on the table. "Here are the phones you wanted. Prepaid with cash and virtually untraceable."

"Good. What else is going on?" Micah seemed to relax with his partner's presence. He sat back down and motioned Troy into one of the remaining chairs.

"I'm trying to get copies of passenger lists from all the planes that flew into and out of Lake Charles on and around the night of the murder. Whoever killed Jason had to have caught a plane back to Kansas City fairly quickly in order to plant that knife in Caylee's apartment."

"What about the security cameras on the ferry?" Micah asked. "Any way to get copies of the recordings for that night?"

Troy shook his head, his blond hair shining in the sunlight. "Not without a warrant, and we don't have the capacity to get one. The cops will be able to look them over, but we won't be able to touch them." He turned his gray eyes on Caylee. "You figured out yet who might be behind this?"

"No."

"She's still insisting nobody she knows is responsible," Micah said, his tone sounding like he thought she might be delusional.

She glared at him. "I'm not crazy," she replied curtly. "I know the people in my life and they just aren't capable of something like this."

"Then we need to look deeper," Troy replied. "Maybe somebody on the periphery of your life."

"Have you learned anything more about Grant Worthington?" Micah asked. "Maybe he could tell us something that was going on in his son's life that would explain this."

"I spoke to him early this morning." Troy frowned. "That man has ice in his veins. Jason's body is barely cold, and Grant was at his office this morning, business as usual. He refused to meet me for an interview, said whatever issues he had with his son were Worthington business and not for public access."

Micah raised a dark eyebrow. "That just whets my appetite to talk to the man."

"Yeah, well that's not going to happen if he has any say in the matter," Troy replied. "The few friends Jason had also aren't talking anymore. Luke contacted a few of those so-called friends this morning, and all they'd tell him was that Jason was a terrific guy and as far as they knew, he wasn't having problems with anyone. I have a feeling Grant or some of his muscle told them not to talk to anyone about Jason."

An overwhelming sense of despair welled up inside Caylee. How was this possibly going to end if they couldn't even figure out a motive or identify a single credible suspect?

"We need a car," Micah said.

Troy sat back and looked at him in surprise. "Why?"

"I don't like being here without an escape. What if something goes wrong? What if the police somehow get wind that we're holed up here? I can run like the wind, but I'm not sure Caylee can run that fast." A touch of dark humor lit Micah's eyes.

"Trust me, if it were a matter of life and death, I could run pretty darned fast," she replied.

"We'll get you a car here later this afternoon," Troy replied.

For the next few minutes the two men talked about Recovery Inc. business. Caylee tuned the conversation out and stared out the window where all evidence of the storm the night before had disappeared.

What was happening at the store? Although Vicki was a decent manager, she didn't always make the best business decisions. Stop worrying, Caylee told herself. The store is in great shape, there's no way it can all go to ruin if you're absent for a couple of days.

She turned her gaze back to Micah. A couple of days. Was it really possible that they could resolve this mess in a couple of days? Somehow she didn't think so.

Her father had raised her to be self-reliant, but she was out of her league here. She was depending on Micah to lead her out of the darkness and back into the light of her life. But somehow she wasn't sure that Micah knew the difference between darkness and light.

All she really knew about him was that he was a man who didn't believe in promises and who seemed to expect that family and or friends could betray him. Just knowing that much about him pulled at her, making her want to dig deeper and discover the source of that darkness.

She frowned. Was she focused on solving the mystery of Micah simply because it seemed much less difficult than solving the mystery that had her hiding out in a safe house, afraid of both the police and a killer?

"We'll get that car here sometime in the next hour or two," Troy said as he rose from the table. As usual, Micah got up to walk him out.

"Thank you, Troy, for everything you're doing for us," she said. She realized how lucky she was to have Micah and his two buddies in her corner. If it hadn't been Micah behind the controls of that plane, she would probably be cooling her heels in jail right now facing a murder trial.

"No problem," Troy replied. "I'll always have Micah's back, just like I know he'll always have mine."

As the two men left the kitchen Caylee leaned back in her chair and thought about the obvious bond that existed between the three men.

She tried to think of a friend who would have her back no matter what the circumstances, and was dismayed to realize she couldn't come up with a single name. Sure, she had the people who worked for her, but they weren't really close friends. Once the shop closed for the day they all went back to their own lives.

"What's wrong?" Micah said as he walked back into the room.

"Nothing, why?"

He leaned a slim hip against the cabinets. "You look sad."

She flashed him a half smile. "Given the circumstances, don't you find it appropriate that I'd feel a bit sad?"

"Of course that's appropriate, but I just got the feeling you were sad about something else."

She leaned back and released a small sigh. "I was just thinking how sad it is that I'm thirty years old and I don't have friends like your Troy and Luke."

His features softened and his lips curved up into one of his devastating smiles. "Few people have friends like *my* Luke and Troy."

"I've been working so hard for the last several years, I haven't formed any kind of real relationships," she said. "The friendships I had before my father died faded when I started working all the time. I think that's why I was so vulnerable to Jason. I had begun to realize that all the friends I used to run around with were married and starting families, and I was ready for that, to find somebody special and share my life with him." She smiled. "Here I go again, talking too much when you didn't even ask me a question."

"It's all right." He returned to his chair at the table, bringing with him that evocative scent of clean male and spice cologne. "I'm starting to get used to it."

"Maybe if you talked more, I'd talk less."

He raised a dark brow. "You promise that would work?" A wicked light of good humor shone from his eyes.

She laughed. "Probably not," she confessed. The brief burst of laughter felt good, releasing some of the tension that had twisted inside her since she'd left the island of Fortuna.

Micah cleared his throat and pulled the notepad he'd been writing in earlier closer to him. "So, did you think of anyone else who might have had a key to your apartment?"

And just that quickly they were back at it, him shooting questions at her like probing bullets and her struggling to make sense of the senseless.

He asked her over and over again about everyone in her life, not just personal relationships but business ones as well. "Is there anyone who has come into your store who seemed odd?" he asked. "A salesman, a customer, anyone?"

"I need my day planner," she said. "It's a history of everything that happens in my life. It's at the store. Maybe we could meet Aunt Patsy somewhere and she can bring it to me."

It was around three when Troy and Luke dropped off a car. They didn't come inside, simply handed Micah the keys to the sedan, then left once again.

Micah returned to drilling Caylee until dinnertime. They stopped to eat a meal of hamburgers and chips, and afterward Caylee refused to answer another question.

"I've had it," she said as they went into the living room and she flopped down on the sofa. "You've picked and poked my life all day long and I'm still not convinced this is all about me. I mean, maybe somebody wanted Jason dead and I was just a convenient fall guy."

"Maybe," he agreed. "I'll know what was going on in Jason's life by this time tomorrow."

She looked at him in surprise. "How?"

He smiled, only this time there was no warmth, no spark of humor in the gesture. "Because first thing in the morning, I'm going to kidnap Grant Worthington and hold him until we have the answers we need."

Chapter Five

Caylee sat on the sofa in the dark living room, her heart thumping with wild anticipation. Micah thought he was going to get up this morning, slip out of the house and kidnap a man while she remained here and waited for the big, bad ex-SEAL to return.

That wasn't going to happen. There was no way he was leaving her here alone while he attempted to kidnap a prominent citizen off the street. He was crazy to even try such a stunt alone.

They'd argued about it long into the night, her trying to talk him out of it and him as immovable as a boulder in his determination.

"He held Jason's purse strings. He controlled his son and would know more about what was going on in Jason's life than Jason's friends. We have to talk to him," he exclaimed. "He may be the key to us figuring out who wanted his son dead. He might also know of somebody who might want you dead if you hooked up with Jason. And I'm pretty sure Grant

Worthington won't be willing to meet us for lunch to have our little chat."

She'd finally given up trying to talk any sense into him and had gone to bed, but not to sleep. She'd stayed awake all night waiting for the moment he'd get up and leave. Because no matter what he thought to the contrary, he wouldn't be leaving by himself.

As she'd lain awake, she'd realized that it would be fairly easy for Micah to remove himself from Jason's murder. He'd taken the ferry to the island and the security cameras would be time-stamped. He'd immediately gone to the Worthington estate and had gotten into the plane. The timing was off for him to have had time to kill Jason, and he had concrete evidence to create more than a reasonable doubt of his guilt.

He could have thrown her to the wolves at any time since the murder. He'd had permission from the bank that owned the plane to retrieve it so he had a legitimate reason to be on the island.

She'd been the one hiding in the back of the plane, pretending to have a gun. All he would have to do is explain how she'd threatened him for a ride back to Kansas City and he could probably easily clear his name.

There was no way she was going to allow him to take the risk of this kidnapping alone. She'd never been a stand-on-the-sidelines kind of woman, and they were partners in this mess for as long as they were together.

Besides, maybe talking to Grant Worthington was the only way to get some answers.

She heard a sound from the bedroom and her stomach knotted with nervous anxiety as she thought of the day ahead. She was going to take part in kidnapping a man. The whole idea was too crazy to believe.

She straightened on the sofa as she sensed, rather than saw Micah enter the darkened room. "Don't bother trying to sneak out of here without me," she said.

He muttered a curse and she winced against the sudden light as he flipped on the switch. "You scared the hell out of me," he said. "You're lucky I didn't have my gun drawn."

"Sorry, that wasn't my intention," she replied and got up from the sofa. "I just wanted you to understand that you're not doing this by yourself, Micah."

"Don't be stupid, Caylee. There's no reason for you to come with me."

"It only makes sense that two kidnappers are better than one," she said with a forced lightness. He scowled, apparently not amused by her attempt at humor. "Micah, I'm not going to let you do this on your own. We're partners. That means if one of us takes a risk, then we both take the risk. Please, it's the way it should be, the way I want it to be."

She saw his hesitation, his gaze troubled and filled with doubt and she quickly pressed the issue. "I can help," she said. "I can serve as a lookout or a getaway driver, but you have to admit that this is definitely a two-man operation."

"This could all go really badly," he warned.

"I'm already wanted for murder, why not add a little kidnapping charge into the mix?" she replied flippantly.

He shook his head and laughed. It was the first time she'd heard his laughter, and the sound of it shot a shockwave of heat through her, a sexual heat like an electric jolt.

"So, what's the plan?" she asked as she consciously tamped down the crazy, unexpected emotion.

He glanced at his watch, then motioned toward the kitchen. "Come on, we have plenty of time for coffee and toast. I never like to kidnap anyone on an empty stomach."

She followed him to the kitchen table and sat while he made the coffee, then pulled the toaster out from the cabinet and grabbed a couple of pieces of bread.

It wasn't until they each had a cup of coffee and toast in front of them that he joined her at the table and began to lay out his plan.

"I spent most of the night reading everything I could find on Grant Worthington, trying to figure out his routine and find some weak spot in his personal security."

"And what did you find?" She took a bite of her toast and wondered if all kidnappers ate breakfast before committing their crime. The whole thing was surreal. Her entire life had become surreal.

"Our Mr. Worthington is a creature of habit. That works to our advantage. He leaves his house at precisely 5:45 in the morning and goes to a gym near his office. He works out for an hour and returns to his car where his driver is waiting at seven-fifteen. The driver then takes him to his office building two blocks away."

"So, what are you thinking?" She set the toast down, realizing she was far too nervous to eat.

"I'm thinking the best place to take him is as he leaves the gym and before he gets into his car." Micah's eyes were the frost of winter as he looked at her over the rim of his coffee mug.

"What about his driver? Won't he be a problem?"

"Trust me, he won't be a problem."

She stared at him and swallowed around the lump that rose up in her throat. "You aren't going to kill him, are you?"

He took a sip of his coffee and then smiled. "You've been watching too many movies. I would never kill a man unless he was trying to kill me. Trust me, Grant's driver isn't going to be an issue."

Caylee wasn't sure why, but it mattered to her that he had the same kind of moral compass she had. She nearly laughed out loud at the absurdity of her thoughts. They were about to kidnap an influential man and somehow she'd made that all right in her mind.

In a million years, she'd never have guessed that a time would come in her life when that would be acceptable behavior. Apparently her moral compass changed when under pressure. She drew a deep breath. "Does it make us bad people that we're going to do this?" she asked.

Micah's features softened as he gazed at her for a long moment. His hand reached out and touched the back of one of hers. Instantly she turned her hand over and twined her fingers with his, grateful for the physical contact of his warmth against her cold. He had big hands, hands that appeared to be capable of handling anything.

"No," he finally replied. "It doesn't make us bad people. It just makes us desperate people caught up in circumstances that call for desperate measures." He pulled his hand from hers. "Neither one of us asked for this. We just have to figure out a way to get out of it."

She wrapped her fingers around her mug, seeking the warmth of the liquid within, although wishing he were still holding her hand.

"Why don't you just go to the police and tell them I'm the one they're looking for, that all you did was go to retrieve a plane. If you fast-talked enough you could probably easily get yourself out of this mess."

That slow grin curved his sensual lips upward. "Fast-talking is your style, not mine."

"Seriously, Micah, why haven't you just turned on me to get yourself out of all this?" She searched his stern features even though she knew she wouldn't see the answer there.

He was a difficult man to read, his thoughts and emotions were kept close to the vest. She'd only know the answer if he decided to tell her.

"Like you said, we're partners in this. Besides, no matter how fast I talk, it won't keep me out of jail as long as Wendall Kincaid is Chief of Police."

"Why does he hate you so much?"

He frowned and was silent for a long minute, obviously deciding whether he wanted to tell her or not. He released a deep sigh. "Wendall has a sister. She and I met at a fundraiser about six months ago, and she came on hot and heavy. We hooked up that night and she led me to believe she understood that I wasn't looking for a relationship, that it was just a one-night kind of thing."

"But she didn't understand," Caylee said, surprised at a tiny sliver of jealousy that reared its ugly head as she thought of Micah in the arms of another woman. Crazy. The unusual stress was obviously making her more than a little crazy.

His eyes narrowed slightly. "She understood, but she has a mean streak a mile wide. She told her brother I led her on, that I broke her heart. And fool that he is, he believed her. I only knew her for twenty-four hours. A heart can't get broken in that amount of time."

"Depends on the woman, depends on the circumstances," Caylee replied.

"Trust me, she did this just to create drama. Anyway, since then, Wendall has been looking for a reason to screw up my life."

Caylee gave him a sly smile. "That's what you get for running with fast women."

He grunted in what might have been the beginning of another laugh, but it didn't quite materialize. Instead he looked at his watch and his features tightened. "Time to go." He scooted back in the chair. "Last chance to bail out."

She shook her head, although her stomach bucked and jumped with anxiety. "I'm not bailing. If this is going to be done, then we're both going to do it."

"Then let's go." He stood and Caylee did the same, a roar of nerves sounding in her head. She'd have protested the plan if she had any alternative. She'd never have agreed to such drastic measures if things hadn't appeared so bleak for them.

Hopefully a face-to-face meeting with Grant Worthington would provide some information that they could sink their teeth into, something that might point a finger at the real killer.

Surely Grant Worthington wanted to get to the truth of the matter as much as they did. She just hoped he'd forgive them for what they were about to do.

"I'll be right back," Micah said. He went down the hallway to his bedroom and returned a moment later with a small duffel bag. She didn't want to ask what it contained, but her imagination filled it with duct tape, rope and all the accoutrement for kidnapping.

They reached the front door, and she was about to step outside when Micah caught her by the arm and twirled her around. Without warning, he took her in his arms and took her lips with his.

The mouth that looked so stern, so unyielding, plied hers with soft heat, and even though she was shocked by the kiss, she couldn't help but respond. He dizzied her, the scent of him filling her nose as his mouth worked magic against hers.

The kiss was over as fast as it began, leaving her wanting more. He dropped his arms from around her and stepped back.

Caylee reached up and touched her mouth with two fingers. "Why…why did you do that?"

For just a moment his eyes blazed with blue flames as he held her gaze. "In case things go really wrong, I didn't want to have to wonder anymore how you would taste."

Caylee stared at him. For the first time in her life, she was utterly speechless.

HE SHOULDN'T have kissed her. As they walked to the car he cursed himself for his momentary weakness. He needed to be clear-headed and focused on the task ahead, but at the moment it was difficult to concentrate on anything but the warmth of her sweet, full lips lingering on his.

As he'd questioned her the day before, he'd found it increasingly difficult to ignore how much he wanted to kiss her. Maybe it was because she'd looked so sexy in the white shorts and pink T-shirt that intensified the green of her eyes. Or perhaps it was the way her lips would unexpectedly curl into that beautiful smile of hers. Whatever the case, the need to kiss her had been growing for what felt like months.

She got into the passenger side of the car as he threw the small tote bag into the backseat, then slid behind the steering wheel.

Again today she wore shorts that showcased the shapely length of her legs. The yellow T-shirt she wore not only advertised a famous brand name but also high-lighted her dark hair and the vivid green of her eyes.

He tightened his grip on the steering wheel. Dawn was just beginning to peek out of the night sky as they drove away from the house. They would get to the downtown gym early but that's the way Micah wanted it.

"How is this going to work?" Caylee asked as he got on the highway that would lead them to the downtown district.

"We'll park as close as we can to the front door of the gym, then we'll wait while Grant enjoys his morning workout." Micah relaxed his hands on the steering wheel as his mind raced with details. It was getting the details right that made the difference between a successful operation and a catastrophe.

"I can't imagine that Grant's driver will sit the full hour in the confines of the car. There's a coffee shop up the street from the gym. My guess is that the driver will walk up to get a cup of coffee, maybe buy a morning newspaper. Even if he doesn't, I'm banking on the fact that he'll get out of the car to stretch his legs or maybe have a smoke. And when he gets back into the car he'll no longer be alone. I'll be with him."

"And what if he doesn't get out?" she asked worriedly.

"Then I'll figure something out," he replied.

"And where will I be?" she asked.

He flashed her a quick glance, not surprised to see the tension that rode her delicate features. He'd have preferred that she'd stayed at the house and out of harm's way. But he'd seen the determined light in her eyes and figured that her remaining behind wasn't an option.

"You'll be in this car," he explained. "Your job is to follow me. I've got to get Worthington someplace isolated where he and I can talk without distractions."

"I can do that," she replied with an obvious touch of bravado.

"And you are to stay in the car while I question Grant. If something happens and it looks like things are going south, then I want you to drive away and not look back."

She was silent for a moment. "What could go wrong?" she finally asked, a nervous tremor in her voice.

He nearly laughed at the naiveté of her question. What could go wrong? He'd had little time to plan this, had no idea if Grant's driver was armed, if today might be the day Grant changed his routine or his car would break down. There were a hundred variables that could add up to a kidnapping gone wrong, but he didn't want her to know it.

For the next few minutes Micah welcomed her silence as he went into himself to find the cool, calm place he always went to before an operation. It was a place familiar and comfortable, completely detached and without emotion.

Surprisingly, Caylee remained quiet until he parked in front of Joe's Gym, an upscale sportsclub with an unpretentious name. The sun had just begun its upward climb, although it was still too early for the streets to come alive with people.

Micah cut the engine and moved his seat back to give himself more leg room, his head filled with the details he'd gleaned during his night of Internet surfing. It was amazing what could be learned about people in the public eye with a little time and a click of fingers on a keyboard. Frightening, really, how easily information was accessed.

Grant Worthington was a man who loved the spotlight. Micah had found hundreds of newspaper and magazine articles about him. Not only was he touted as an extremely successful businessman, but also a philanthropist who gave back to the community. He and his young, attractive second wife were a frequent topic on the society pages.

Micah had picked through the pieces of the interviews Grant had given and gotten the facts he needed and a picture of the man himself. His impression of Grant was that the man was driven and ruthless in his business dealings and arrogant about his successes.

The only thing he'd been unable to get a handle on was how Grant would react to his own kidnapping. And it was that little fact that worried him.

"Where are your mother and father, Micah?"

He started, for a moment he'd been so lost in his thoughts he'd forgotten Caylee was in the car with him. He looked at her, surprised by her question.

"You think because you have me captive in a car you can ask me personal questions?" he asked.

She flashed him a nervous grin. "If you prefer, I can fill the waiting time by telling you everything I know about diamonds and other fine gems, although I'll let you know ahead of time the conversation is going to be pretty boring unless you're a gemologist." She paused a moment. "Besides, I figured now that you've kissed me, I'm allowed to ask you a personal question or two."

"I don't know where my parents are," he replied. "I never knew my father, and my mother left me when I was eight." He tried to ignore the tiny knot that clenched in his stomach.

"Left you? What do you mean she left you? With family? With friends?" Her eyes glowed luminous in the dawn light.

"On a park bench in the rain." He frowned, wondering what it was about her that had pulled the words out of him?

Maybe it was because she'd been so free and open in sharing her life with him.

"I don't understand. What do you mean she left you on a park bench in the rain?"

Micah stared out the front window, wishing he hadn't given them so much time to sit and wait, wishing he hadn't opened up this particular can of worms. His past was something he never talked about, something he tried not to think about. Still, as Caylee reached over and placed her warm hand on his, it was as if her touch opened the locked box of his past.

"Like I said, I never knew my dad. I'm not sure my mom knew who fathered me. It was just mom and me, and she had problems. We drifted from place to place, her from man to man. I realize now she was an alcoholic who abused drugs, but as a kid I didn't know what was going on with her. I just knew that my life was different than other kids'."

Caylee's hand tightened on his, as if she could feel the knot of tension that twisted inside him, as if she understood the emotion that rose up to fill the back of his throat. But, of course she couldn't understand. She'd grown up with loving family members surrounding her. He'd had nobody.

"One day she got me up and told me I didn't have

to go to school, that she'd planned a special day at the park with me." Micah frowned. Funny how that day was burned so brightly in his memory. "I had a bad feeling from the moment she woke me up. She was manic happy and when we got to the park she told me how much she loved the new guy in her life, that finally she was going to get what she wanted, and nobody and nothing was going to stand in her way." He turned and forced a smile. "I guess I was in her way."

He pulled his hand from hers and checked his watch. Worthington should be showing up within the next twenty minutes. He didn't need to be thinking about that day so long ago. He should be focused on the mission ahead. But now that he'd begun the story the rest of it pressed to be released.

He drew a deep breath. "I didn't want to be in the park. It was a crappy day, overcast and threatening rain. I wanted to be in school or in the motel room where we'd been staying for a while. It was about noon when she told me to sit on the bench and she was going to get me an ice cream cone. She promised she'd be right back." He swallowed against the rise of emotion.

"But she never came back," Caylee said softly.

"It started to thunder and lightning, but I didn't move from that bench. It began to rain, but I stayed where I was because she'd promised she was coming back." He could still remember how frightened he'd been as the thunder had boomed and lightning had sizzled in the air. It wasn't until he'd been soaked through and the storm began to pass that he realized she wasn't coming back for him.

"What happened after that?" Caylee's voice once again pulled him back to the present.

"A policeman found me and took me to the station. That night I entered the foster care system."

"Please tell me you had a wonderful foster family." Her hope for him was evident in her voice.

He smiled at her, the ball of tension inside him dissipating from his sheer willpower alone. "They all might have been nice families, but I wasn't such a nice kid. I was pissed off at the world and I went out of my way to make everyone's lives miserable. I was moved from place to place until I got to high school. I was a real tough guy, picking fights, always one step away from real trouble. Then a coach challenged me to channel my energy into sports. It changed my life. After high school I signed up for the Navy and never looked back."

"And you never saw your mother again?" Caylee's expression was soft, far too appealing.

"Never wanted to," he replied and once again directed his attention out the car window. "The Navy became my family, along with Troy and Luke. They're all I need as far as family is concerned."

He straightened up in his seat as a black limo pulled to the curb directly in front of the gym door. "There they are," he said, grateful to leave thoughts of his miserable past behind and focus on this moment and the mission ahead.

He could feel Caylee's tension wafting in the car interior, but he didn't look at her. He remained totally focused on the car that held their quarry.

The back door opened, and Grant Worthington stepped out. Good, Micah thought, he hadn't waited for his driver to get out and open the door for him.

Grant Worthington was tall and in good physical shape for a sixty-year-old man. He looked neither left nor right as he headed for the front door of the gym. When he disappeared inside, Caylee released an audible sigh.

"Now we see how easy Grant Worthington's driver is going to make this for us," Micah murmured.

He and Caylee watched the car in silence for fifteen minutes before the driver got out of the car. He was a thin man, not young. Micah guessed the man would prove no problem.

The driver stretched, lit a cigarette and then began to amble down the street toward the coffee shop. Micah turned to Caylee.

"This is where we part ways. Remember, just follow that car, and when we get to where we're going, you stay in this car. If anything goes wrong or I give you a signal, you drive the hell out of there." Before she could say another word, he grabbed the small tote bag from the backseat, got out of the car and followed the driver.

Chapter Six

Madness. Caylee got out of the passenger seat and got in behind the steering wheel, wondering how she'd ever agreed to such madness.

She was a thirty-year-old shopkeeper, for God's sake. A woman who'd always tried to do the right thing, who paid her taxes on time and had never even gotten a speeding ticket. And now she was part of a kidnapping scheme.

She grabbed hold of the steering wheel with both hands as Micah disappeared into the coffee shop. She hoped this was worth it. She hoped this didn't just increase the criminal charges against them without getting them some answers.

She really hoped that Grant Worthington would forgive them for this if they were able to find the person responsible for his son's death. Who had killed Jason? And why had they put the murder weapon in her apartment if not to frame her for his murder?

Glancing around, she saw that nobody was paying

any attention to her. She didn't appear to be drawing unwanted notice from anyone.

The minutes ticked by agonizingly slowly and as she waited, Micah's words replayed in her mind. Poor little boy. What must it do to a person's psyche when the one who should love you the best just walks away?

Although Caylee had lost her mother at a young age, she'd always known that it hadn't been her mother's choice to leave them behind. And Caylee had never doubted the depths of her father's love for her. But Micah had grown up with nobody.

He was the kind of man who would hate her sympathy, but she couldn't help but feel sorry for the little boy he'd been, a little boy who had grown up not believing in promises because the most important person in his life had broken her promise to him.

All thoughts of Micah as a little boy shot out of her head as he and Grant Worthington's driver stepped out of the coffee shop. At a glance, they looked like two buddies enjoying one another's company. Micah's arm was around the slender man's shoulder and he was smiling as if all was right with the world.

It was only upon further inspection as they walked closer that she could see the strain on the driver's slender face, the death grip he held on his plastic coffee cup. God, she hadn't wanted to scare anyone, but it was obvious the poor man was terrified.

She wanted to jump out of the car and call the

whole thing off, to tell the driver to get back in his car and go on with his day as usual. But another part of her knew they were running out of options.

She grabbed the steering wheel so tightly her knuckles turned white as she saw the driver get into the driver's seat and Micah get into the door just behind him.

Too late now, she told herself. It was too late to turn back. Micah was in position and all they had to do was wait for Grant Worthington to finish his morning workout.

Once again the minutes passed with excruciating slowness. She kept her attention divided equally between the car in front of her and the door of the gym, dreading the moment when Grant would walk out, yet wanting this whole ordeal to be over.

She thought of her Aunt Patsy. The poor woman must be sick with worry by now. Hopefully at some point this afternoon if she and Micah weren't in jail, she could call her and let her know she was okay, at least for the moment.

Finally, Grant burst out of the doors, his steel gray hair still damp, and a navy blue gym bag clutched in his hand. He looked neither left nor right, but grabbed hold of the back door of his car, opened it and disappeared inside. Caylee started her car and held her breath.

For a moment nothing happened. Her anxiety screamed inside her. Was there a struggle going on inside the car? Was everything about to explode in their faces?

A deep breath of air whooshed out of her as Grant's car roared to life and pulled away from the curb. She followed, her heart pounding painfully in her chest.

It was done. She was now officially an accessory to kidnapping. As she followed through the early morning traffic, she wondered what they were saying inside the car, wondered if they were speaking at all?

She hoped Micah had assured both the driver and Grant that they meant them no harm, that they just needed to get some answers.

The good thing about Kansas City was that from almost any point in the city, if you drove fifteen or twenty minutes you could be out in farmland. Even the Kansas City International Airport was out in the middle of cornfields.

That's where the car headed, to the middle of nowhere. Caylee followed as closely as possible as they left the city, terrified that she might lose sight of them and would not only put Micah in danger, but she'd never be able to find her way back to the safe house.

Grant's car finally pulled to a stop in a field where not a house was in sight and all three men stepped out of the car. Although Micah didn't hold a gun in his hand, he must have let them know that he was armed, for they seemed to be obeying him. He did have the small duffel he'd carried with him when they'd left the house in one hand.

Caylee put the car in park and rolled down her window so she could hear what was going on, but the breeze snatched their words away from her.

She couldn't stand it, not being able to hear, not knowing what was going on. This was as much her life as it was Micah's.

Even though he'd told her to wait in the car, she opened the door and got out. She wanted to look Grant Worthington in the eye and tell him she hadn't killed his son. It was important to her.

As she approached all three men turned to look at her, Grant and the driver with curiosity and Micah with an angry gaze that should have frozen her in her tracks, but didn't.

"Mr. Worthington," she said as she reached where they stood. She studiously kept her gaze away from Micah and instead focused on the father of the man she'd been dating. "My name is Caylee Warren. I was dating your son at the time of his death."

"I know who you are. I've seen your picture splashed all over the news." He looked from Caylee back to Micah. "Now, you want to tell me what this is all about? I'm a busy man," he said with a touch of arrogance.

"My partner tried to set up an interview with you, but you blew him off," Micah said.

"I didn't kill your son," Caylee said. She wanted to grab him by the arm, force him to believe her, but she knew better than to get too close. She didn't want to become a hostage by letting him grab her. "I don't know who did, but it wasn't me. You've got to talk to the authorities, tell them they're looking for the wrong people."

"We want to know if there was anyone Jason was having problems with, if he owed money or was into drugs? Something that would explain what happened," Micah said.

Grant's gray eyes gave nothing away of his inner thoughts. "You two have a lot of nerve, pulling a stunt like this."

"We need some answers," Caylee exclaimed. "And we didn't know how to get them any other way."

"And what makes you think I have any answers for you?" For the first time Grant's features twisted with emotion. "My son was a waste of oxygen, spoiled by the overindulgence of his mother, my first wife. I have little time for fools, and my son was a fool." He smiled at Caylee. "Ah, I see by the expression on your face that my words surprise you. I'm not one of those who subscribe to the notion that you shouldn't speak ill of the dead. My son was weak and pathetic." A whisper of something deeper, the darkness of grief flashed in his eyes. It was there only a moment, then gone. "He was my only child."

"Then help us find out who killed him," Micah said.

"Did he have another girlfriend? Somebody who might have seen me as a threat?" Caylee asked.

Grant offered her a tight smile. "Any woman that

was in Jason's life would have seen *him* as the threat. From what I understand, my son didn't understand the meaning of no. He saw a woman he wanted, and went after her with a single-mindedness that would have made him a tremendous businessman had that energy been directed into something more positive."

"We heard through the grapevine that you'd threatened him with disinheritance if he didn't marry," Micah said. "Maybe you didn't like the idea of your son hooking up with a jewelry clerk?"

One of Grant's eyebrows rose. "You think I killed my own son because I didn't like his choice of partners? Don't be ridiculous. I didn't care who my son hooked up with. I just wanted him to settle down, start a family, become responsible." He looked at his watch and frowned. "Look, I'm going to be late for a meeting if you don't get me back to my office."

Caylee wondered how many of Jason's problems came from the fact that his father appeared to be a cold bastard ruled only by business.

"So you won't help us," Micah said, his tone thick with frustration.

Grant heaved a deep sigh. "Mr. Stone, you don't understand. I *can't* help you. I can't imagine why anyone would kill my son. Nobody stood to gain anything by his death. I don't know what happened. I can't help you. I told Chief Kincaid that I didn't think you two were responsible, but he's certainly not listening to me. Now, are we done here?"

"Are you going to turn us in?" The words blurted from Caylee. "We didn't want to hurt you, but we were desperate to talk to you, to talk to anyone who might be able to tell us something that would point to who killed Jason. We can't get ourselves out of trouble unless we can find the killer."

"You both took a big chance bringing me out here. I could call Chief Kincaid the minute I get back to my office and file a kidnapping report." Caylee held her breath at his words. "But I won't," he continued. "I like initiative and risk-takers and if you two were locked up, then the real killer might never be found." He looked at his watch once again. "I'll give you two five minutes to get out of here, then Raymond will take me back to my office and we'll all pretend this never happened."

Micah grabbed her firmly by the arm and led her back to their car. "Get in," he said tersely as he threw the duffel into the backseat. She hurried to the passenger side as he slid in behind the wheel. He slammed the car into gear and they took off, their tires burning rubber as they hit the main road.

"I told you to stay in the car," he said as he glanced in the rearview mirror.

"I needed to see him face to face, to tell him that I didn't kill his son," she replied. She buckled her seat belt as he hit the highway that would eventually take them back to the safe house. "What's in the bag you brought with you?" she asked.

He cast her a heavy-lidded glance. "The usual tools for torture in case they didn't want to talk." She gasped and a tight grin stretched his lips. "Just kidding. All that's in there is a length of rope and some duct tape in case I needed to tie up the driver."

Just as she'd suspected. "Do you think they'll turn us in?"

"I don't know." A muscle knotted in Micah's jaw. "I won't feel comfortable until we're back at the house. Time will tell if we just added another criminal charge to our records." His jaw throbbed like something was trapped beneath his skin.

His tension filled Caylee. Had they just made a tremendous mistake? Grant hadn't given them anything that might help their case. The entire interview had been worth nothing, except perhaps another twenty years in a jail cell.

She fought against a wave of depression. She'd been trying so hard to hold it all together, but at this moment, things appeared as hopeless as they could get.

Just to prove that things could get worse, a siren began to sound from someplace behind them.

MICAH SWALLOWED A CURSE as he saw the cherry swirl of a police car approaching in the rearview mirror. A weary resignation filled him. Apparently Grant had made a phone call and turned them in.

"I won't run," he said. "Police chases never end well." He glanced over at Caylee, surprised to realize he wished he'd had more time with her. Maybe it had been the kiss that had him thinking such crazy thoughts, or maybe it was simply because he'd prefer to spend more time with her than time behind bars.

The siren grew so loud it was impossible to hear her reply. He pulled the car to the shoulder, a sick feeling in the pit of his stomach.

The patrol car whizzed by them and on down the highway.

"I think I'm going to throw up," Caylee exclaimed.

Micah shot her a quick glance. Her face was blanched of color and a sheen of perspiration dotted her forehead. "Put your head between your knees and take a couple of deep breaths," he said as he pulled back on the highway.

He didn't care if she puked in the car. He was getting them back to the house as soon as possible. After a moment or two, she raised her head and sat back, a bit of color returning to her cheeks.

"I thought our goose was cooked for sure," she said. "I've never been so scared in my life." She expelled another deep breath, her energy suddenly filling the close confines of the car.

It was an energy he understood, had felt a million times himself after a successful mission. It was when the taste of disaster lingered in your mouth for too long, then miraculously disappeared.

He even felt it now, the euphoric high of the cruiser passing them by, of safety after the certainty of catastrophe. Still, he didn't breathe easy until they pulled up in front of the house and got out of the car.

"We'll know by the evening news if Worthington turned us in," he said as he unlocked the front door.

"I don't think he will," she replied. "He said he wouldn't and I believe him."

"Do you believe everything anyone tells you?" he asked as they stepped into the house.

"Until they give me a reason not to believe them," she replied. She walked over to the sofa, and he tried not to watch the sway of her hips beneath the tight shorts. "So, what happens now?" She sat on the sofa and he joined her there.

He swiped a hand through his hair and tried not to focus on the scent of her perfume or the fact that just moments before, when he'd thought they'd been about to be arrested, he'd wished he could kiss her again. "We didn't get anything from Worthington, so that takes us back to square one."

"And what's square one?"

"That this is about you, not Jason."

She held up her hands and shook her head. "I'm not answering any more questions today. We've been through it all, talked about everyone in my life."

"We have to go through it all again," he replied. "We've obviously missed something." His energy level was still peaked by the events of the morning. He got up from the sofa, strung too taut to sit, and finding her nearness too evocative.

Under normal circumstances he'd call Heidi and meet with her for a quick physical release of tension. Heidi knew he was incapable of giving anything meaningful to anyone. She was one of the 'fast' women in his life, who expected nothing from him, and more importantly, didn't want anything from him.

He began to pace back and forth in front of the sofa, trying to stay focused on Jason's murder, but finding it difficult to keep his thoughts off Caylee and that kiss they'd shared.

"I want to see my Aunt Patsy," she said, breaking into his thoughts. "We managed to get out of the house today, so we can set something up to meet her."

"Not today," he replied. "Until we know for sure that Grant isn't turning the heat up on us, we're not leaving this house again."

"If there's nothing on the news about the kidnapping tonight, then can I set up a meeting with her tomorrow?"

Micah stopped pacing to look at her. "Why a meeting? Why not just a phone call to let her know you're all right?"

A dainty frown tugged her eyebrows together and she got up from the sofa, as if she, too, was too full of energy to remain seated. "First and foremost, I want her to bring me my day planner. I have tons of information in that book that might provide the answer we're looking for. Secondly, I *need* to see her in person. I need to hug her, but more importantly I need her to hug me." She took several steps toward Micah. "In fact, I'm desperately in need of a hug right now."

There it was again, her simple declaration of what she needed. And without his volition, his arms opened to her. She flew to him and pressed herself against his chest, her arms circling his waist as his wrapped around her.

She trembled against him, and he recognized how much she was in over her head in all of this. He'd been in tough situations before, but she'd probably never been involved in anything close to this kind of drama. She'd been remarkably clear-headed and calm throughout the ordeal. He just hoped she didn't fall apart now.

As if in answer to his fear, her trembling stopped, but she didn't move out of his arms. Instead she burrowed closer, and Micah felt himself responding to her intimate nearness.

"I could stay here forever," she said softly.

Micah tensed, finding her presence in his arms far too appealing, especially as she pressed closer against him.

Just as he was about to push her away, she raised her head and looked at him, her green eyes smoky with desire. "I want you to make love to me, Micah."

Her words sent an electric arc through him because he couldn't remember the last time he'd wanted a woman as much as he wanted her at this moment.

But he also knew that Caylee was functioning on residual adrenaline and couldn't be thinking clearly. Besides, she wasn't the type of woman he normally hooked up with. She was far too trusting, far too naive. There wasn't a fast bone in her body.

He dropped his arms from around her, but she didn't release her hold on him. "Caylee, that really isn't a good idea," he said, his voice deeper than usual.

"Why not? I want you and you want me."

It was impossible for him to deny his desire with her standing so close to him, close enough to feel that desire for her. "I told you I only hook up with fast women."

"I've just participated in a kidnapping and I'm wanted for murder. How much faster do you want?" she replied.

A laugh escaped him. He wanted to explain, but at that moment she reached up and pressed her warm lips against the underside of his jaw. That simple action unleashed a storm inside him, and he slammed his mouth to hers, giving in to his desire.

She responded with a hunger that stunned him, opening her mouth to him as she molded her body to his. She tasted like a fast woman, hot and eager, not just yielding to him, but taking from him, too.

She touched his tongue with hers, deepening the kiss to the point where he feared there would be no return. He tore his mouth away, needing to stop this now, before she made a mistake, before *they* made a mistake.

"Caylee," he said, the word half spoken, half groaned. "You don't want to do this."

"Don't tell me what I want and what I don't want," she replied, her voice husky and low. "I don't expect you to make me any promises, Micah. Hopefully in a matter of days this will all be behind us, and you'll be part of the adventure I'll think about when I'm back to my normal, boring life. But right now I want you, Micah. Please make love to me."

She stepped back from him, took his hand and began to lead him down the hall toward her bedroom. Somewhere in the back of his mind, Micah knew he should protest, knew that this was probably a bad thing. But, at the moment, the want he saw in her eyes and the flush of heat that filled his veins shouted louder than any of his objections.

When they reached her room, she didn't hesitate. She turned to face him and pulled the bright yellow T-shirt over her head. His gaze automatically went to the white, lacy bra that barely contained her full breasts.

He mirrored her action, pulling off his own T-shirt and tossing it to the floor. No promises, she'd said. That was all he'd needed to hear to make this all okay. As long as she understood the rules, then there would be no repercussions.

He took her back in his arms, loving the way her bare skin felt against his, loving the scent that drifted from her skin, from her hair.

They kissed for what seemed like an eternity. He loved the taste of her. Not just of her mouth, but also the slender curve of her neck, the flesh just behind her ear. His hands moved to her breasts, cupping the fullness through their lacy confines. His thumbs raked over her nipples, hard and eagerly pressing against her bra.

She moaned, a deep, low sound that heated his blood even more. She stumbled back from him, her chest heaving and her eyes glowing primal. Her fingers fumbled with the button of her jeans, and as she pulled them off, he did the same, grabbing his wallet from his back pocket, then kicking off his jeans.

They fell on the bed together, arms and legs tangling as a wildness seemed to grip them both. Her voracity stunned him, excited him to a near fever pitch. It didn't take him long to want her naked, without the minuscule cover of her panties and bra.

Caressing up the silky length of her leg, he drew a deep breath, needing to slow down his raging desire. Otherwise he'd be finished before they'd really begun.

There was a part of him that wanted to be a selfish lover, to take what he needed from her without any thought of what she might need or want from him. If he was selfish and demanding, she wouldn't want to repeat this, and he'd be safe from her ever wanting him again.

But that wasn't who he was at his core. As much

as Micah loved his pleasure, he loved giving his partner pleasure more. He flicked his tongue against one of her pebbly-hard nipples, and she gasped and grabbed his shoulders in a tight grip.

His fingers found the center of her, and she arched to meet his intimate touch. Her breaths came in short, quick pants, and he loved the sound of her rising excitement.

The sunshine flooding in through the windows loved her skin, painting it in golden tones as she moved more frantically against him, her eyes closed and her head thrown back.

He knew the moment she reached her peak, felt her muscles tightening. Her eyes flashed open and pierced into his, and for a suspended moment in time he felt a connection he'd never felt before. Then her entire body shuddered with release, and she closed her eyes again and moaned.

Before the moan had completely stilled in the air, she reached down and touched him, her eyes glittering with a new hunger.

The warmth of her hand around his hardness sent him nearly over the edge. He rolled away from her and grabbed his wallet and pulled out a condom. Making love to her was probably a mistake, but making love to her without protection could prove disastrous.

"Let me," she whispered and took the wrapper from him. She tore it open and pulled out the sheath, then rolled it onto him. By the time she was finished he throbbed with need.

She rolled over on her back and held out her arms to welcome him into her. He entered her with a groan. He trembled with pleasure, surrounded by her moist heat.

He began to move against her, into her, stroking slowly as he gazed down at her face. Nothing that had passed before mattered. Nothing that might happen in the future mattered. He was lost in this moment with this woman.

As he felt the rising tide of his own release moving closer, threatening to drown him, he moved faster, more frantically into her. She clung to him, her long legs wrapping around him, her hands clutching his shoulders as they moved together in a frenzy.

She cried out and every muscle in her body froze, then shuddered and in that moment the tide swept over him and he uttered a deep moan as he drowned in pleasure so intense it stole his breath.

He collapsed just to the side of her, the adrenaline that had pumped through him since the moment he'd opened his eyes that morning now gone.

She leaned up on one elbow, a soft smile playing on her features. "I'd forgotten how nice it could be."

"That was better than nice." He reached up and tucked a strand of her hair behind her ear. "Been a long time for you?"

"An eternity. Just after my father died five years ago. Unfortunately, that relationship didn't last. It was driven by my grief, and once the grief began to pass I realized I wasn't in love."

She placed a hand on his chest and smiled again. "But, I'd forgotten how nice it is to be close to another person, to have that moment when you're so tangled together you aren't sure which arms and legs are your own, and it doesn't matter, when you lose that sense of self and become a part of something bigger."

"Sounds too deep for me," he exclaimed, then stifled a yawn with the back of his hand.

"You're tired," she said, stating the obvious. "So am I." She laid her head back on the pillow next to his. "I don't think I got any sleep at all last night. I was so worried about the whole kidnapping thing. Why don't we just take a little nap?"

"You go ahead and sleep," he said, moving from beneath her hand to sit on the edge of the bed. He stood and walked out of the room and into the bathroom, needing to escape both her presence and the overwhelming desire he had to curl up next to her.

When he returned to the bedroom a moment later for his clothes, she was curled up on her side beneath the sheet. She gave him a sleepy smile and patted the bed next to her. "Come on, Micah, take a nap with me. You'll feel better after an hour or so of sleep."

As if he was no longer in control of his own body,

his feet moved him toward the bed. She was right, he could use an hour or so of sleep. He'd been up most of the night as well, worrying about the kidnapping, going over everything in his mind.

He slid back into bed, and instantly she spooned him, settling her pert butt against him as if that's where she belonged.

Dropping an arm around her slender waist, he realized that if he allowed it, this woman could be far more dangerous than anything Chief Kincaid might have planned for him.

Chapter Seven

Caylee awoke with the new dawn light streaking through the bedroom window. She wasn't surprised to find herself alone in the bed. After they'd napped the day before, they'd gotten up and eaten dinner, then Caylee had called her Aunt Patsy and set up a meeting for this afternoon.

She wasn't sure whether the little tremor of excitement that raced through her was because she was going to see her aunt today or a residual emotion from making love with Micah.

She rolled over on her back and stared up at the ceiling, her thoughts racing back to those moments with Micah. She'd had a feeling he'd be an amazing lover and she hadn't been wrong.

He brought his personal intensity to the act and had made her feel as if she were the most important person on the face of the earth.

But she knew that was nothing but an illusion. She told herself that her white-hot desire for him had been driven by the unusually heightened energy that had coursed through her after the kidnapping. She'd wanted, needed a connection that spoke of life, and she was sure he'd been driven by the same forces.

Still, there had been a single moment when their gazes had locked, when she'd seen a whisper of vulnerability in his eyes. For just that moment she'd wanted to wrap him up in her arms and hold him in a place where nobody would ever hurt him again.

Crazy. She'd be crazy to believe that what they'd shared meant anything to him other than a hard, fast release of tension. She had to remember that they were really nothing more than two strangers thrown together by circumstances beyond their control.

He'd made it clear that he liked fast women, and even though she'd acted like one the day before, at heart she wasn't a fast woman at all. She wanted love and passion in her life, but she also needed promises and a commitment to be truly happy.

She rolled out of bed and grabbed a clean pair of shorts and a T-shirt, then raced across the hall into the bathroom. The scent of coffee chased her, letting her know that Micah was already up and about.

Moments later she stood beneath a hot spray of water and tried not to think about those moments in Micah's arms. She didn't want to like him. That first night in the plane she'd been certain she didn't like him, but her attitude toward him had changed since then.

There were flashes of his sense of humor, hints of

a deeply hidden warmth that she found intoxicating. He was like a surprise wrapped in layer after layer of paper. Each layer torn away revealed a new dimension that only whetted her appetite to get to the next layer.

She turned off the shower, grabbed her towel and turned her thoughts to the day ahead. The evening news hadn't mentioned new charges being filed against her and Micah. In fact, with a new murder in the headlines and a missing mother of three young children to report, the story of Jason's murder and the hunt for them hadn't made the news at all.

She'd phoned Aunt Patsy and told her only that she was fine and she'd explain everything today when they met at a special place Patsy had taken her and her cousin Rick as children. She'd asked her aunt to get her day planner from Vicki, her store manager, and bring it with her, then had hung up with Patsy sputtering questions.

She dressed quickly, then left the bathroom and went in search of Micah. She found him seated at the kitchen table, a cup of coffee in front of him as he stared out the window where the morning light competed with a thickening of rain clouds. She stood for a moment, watching him as he gazed outside, seemingly unaware of her presence.

God he was attractive. And part of that was his lack of self-awareness. Those broad shoulders had felt wonderful beneath her fingers the night before and his dark curly hair was like silk.

"You going to stand there all morning or are you going to sit down?" he said without shifting his gaze.

"How did you do that?" she asked as she walked over to the coffeemaker. "You didn't even look at me. How did you know I was there?"

He turned and offered her a sly grin. "I'm an ex-Navy SEAL. I'm trained to have a sixth sense about these things." His smile deepened. "Besides, I saw your reflection in the window."

She laughed and poured herself a cup of coffee, then joined him at the table. "And here I thought it was some sort of macho skill you picked up along the way."

His smile faded as he looked back toward the window. "I hope our plans to meet your aunt today don't get rained out. The weatherman is calling for more storms this afternoon."

"Nothing short of a tornado is going to keep me from meeting with Aunt Patsy," she replied. "I need an Aunt Patsy hug."

"She gives good ones?"

"The best. Everyone should have an Aunt Patsy in their lives. I practically lived with her and Rick during the summers. Dad would drop me off there in the mornings on his way to the store, then pick me up at bedtime. I'm talking too much, aren't I?"

He smiled again. "It's all right. I'm actually kind of enjoying it." He took a sip of his coffee, then looked at her again. "Is there an uncle to go with Aunt Patsy?"

"No, he died when Rick was two."

"So how does Aunt Patsy support herself?"

"Uncle Ben left her with a sizable insurance set-
tlement and she invested wisely. Money has never
seemed to be an issue, although she isn't extravagant
with it." She frowned. "She has no motive for
wanting me gone, Micah. She's one of the most
centered, happy-go-lucky people I know. She loves
me. People who love you don't try to hurt you."

The gray of the morning clouds seemed to creep
into his eyes. He took another sip of his coffee,
then placed the cup back on the table. "Jason's
funeral is today."

Unexpected grief ripped through Caylee. Even
though she'd disliked Jason and had found him
weird, she grieved not only for his untimely, violent
death, but also, selfishly, for the loss of her own life
as she knew it.

"Hopefully most of the police force will be at the
funeral and not following your Aunt Patsy when she
leaves her house this afternoon," he continued.

"Surely the police won't know that she's leaving
to meet us."

"Unless they're tapping her phone."

Caylee sat back in her chair. "Can they do that?"

"I wouldn't put anything past Kincaid," he replied.

"Aunt Patsy is smart. If she thinks she's being
followed she won't show up. Hopefully that won't
happen. I'd like to get my hands on my day planner.

I write everything down in it, every name of anyone I meet or see during the day. Maybe I'll see the name of somebody I haven't been able to think of."

"We need something to happen. I've got a life to get back to," he said.

She wanted to ask him what kind of life. It was obvious he had his work, but he didn't seem to have anything or anyone else. But, she didn't ask. He looked closed off, teetering on a foul mood and she didn't want to upset him further by poking and prying.

The morning passed slowly with an uneasy air between them. Micah remained curt and distant. She had a feeling he was drawing boundaries after crossing over them so completely the day before, letting her know in a passive-aggressive way that even though he'd made love to her he was only here with her because he preferred it to jail.

She got the message and felt a rising irritation of her own. What was he afraid of, that she'd become a stalker girlfriend? That she'd demand an engagement ring and a walk down the aisle just because they'd slept together?

Troy stopped by at noon and told them he and Luke were going to attend Jason's funeral and be their eyes there. "If anyone acts strangely, we'll see it," he said. "If anything is said that points a finger at somebody, we'll hear it. Kincaid is smart; he'll know we're there on Micah's behalf, but he won't be able to do anything about it. Meanwhile we've done all we can to check into his background. No evidence of drug-abuse although he liked his booze."

He focused his attention on Caylee. "It is true, you know. Often the murderer is among the grieving at the funeral of the victim."

Caylee nodded. She was grateful they hadn't given up on the notion that it had been somebody in Jason's life who had killed him, not somebody in hers.

When Troy finally left, it was time for Caylee and Micah to go meet Patsy. Excitement mingled with apprehension as she got in the passenger seat of the car.

She knew it was always dangerous when they chose to leave the house, that a simple traffic stop could mean disaster for them both.

As much as she wanted her day planner, and as eager as she was to see her aunt Patsy, she knew they were taking a huge chance by meeting her in a public place. If Kincaid had wiretapped Patsy's phone, then he would know that at some point today Patsy intended to meet with them. Although she'd told Micah that her aunt would be careful, it was possible Patsy would never know there was a tail on her.

"The park is just off Antioch and Vivion Road," she said as he pulled out of the driveway. "It's called Penguin Park. There's a huge Penguin slide that stands in the center. The park was a favorite place for us to come when I was young. Rick always loved the slide and I loved the swings."

"Parks have never been my favorite places,"

Micah replied, reminding her of his childhood trauma. "If I don't like the way things look when we get there, we aren't getting out of the car."

She nodded her agreement. She wanted to see her Aunt Patsy, but not at the expense of their freedom or their lives.

"I'll do whatever you want me to do," she said. "I bow to your superior knowledge in these matters," she added in an attempt to alleviate some of the tension.

For an instant the cool distance he'd maintained all morning slipped and he offered her a flash of a grin. "I imagine you as a woman who doesn't bow to anyone too often."

"I've had to be fairly tough to manage my business as successfully as I have. Besides, if I was easily cowed I would have never climbed out that bathroom window in Fortuna and run."

"And if you hadn't climbed out of that window then it might have been your funeral taking place this afternoon."

His words sobered her, bringing home the fact once again that the intended victim in Fortuna might not have been Jason at all.

"If that's the case, then you aren't just protecting me from incarceration for a crime I didn't commit. You might be protecting me from somebody who wants to kill me."

This time when he gazed at her his eyes were once again frosted. "What makes you think I'm protecting you at all? I just want to clear my own name. You happen to be along for the ride."

She stared at him as he directed his attention back out the car window. "You know, you don't have to be mean to me to prove a point."

A ruddy color crept up his neck. "I don't know what you're talking about."

"You've been irritable all morning and I think it's because of what happened yesterday. You don't have to remind me that making love didn't mean anything. I'm not going to become a stalker or tell the Chief of Police that you took advantage of me. And I think it's pretty arrogant of you to think that just because we went to bed together I might do something stupid like fall in love with you."

To his credit he managed to look slightly sheepish. "I just want to make sure we're on the same page, that you understand that I'm not looking for a relationship."

"I got it," she replied with a touch of her own irritation. "You don't have to hammer me over the head with your attitude."

She fell silent and directed her gaze out the window where the skies were getting darker by the minute. The sun that had peeked out earlier had fled beneath the dark, angry clouds that had taken over.

She sat up straighter as the park came into view. The penguin that was the namesake of the park rose up above all the other playground equipment. A happy smile competed with his bright red bowtie and a slide flew down from his rotund chest.

This had been their favorite place to spend an afternoon when she and Rick were children. Many a picnic lunch had been eaten at the wooden tables on the outskirts of the playground with the penguin smiling benevolently over their heads.

This had been a place of happiness for Caylee, and she desperately hoped that after today it would remain that way in her memory.

No other cars were in the parking lot as Micah pulled in. It appeared they had the place to themselves. As he shut off the car, she unbuckled her seat belt, surprised at the flutter of anxiety that disturbed her tummy.

She hoped this wasn't a mistake. She hoped that the bad feeling that suddenly gripped her was nothing more than her lunch lying heavy in her gut. She tucked a strand of her hair behind her ear and hoped she hadn't led them into disaster.

MICAH DIDN'T LIKE staying in the car. He felt like they were a couple of sitting ducks made vulnerable by the car windows on all four sides.

"I still don't see why we had to have a face-to-face meeting," he said as he gazed across the small park to the wooded area on the other side.

"Micah, you may not need anyone in your life, but the people in mine are important to me. I know my

Aunt Patsy, and no phone call was going to assure her that I was really all right. For her to know for sure that I'm okay she needs to see for herself. Besides, I want my day planner."

He swallowed a sigh and wondered if she'd ever given a one-sentence reply to a question in her life? He glanced at his watch. They were supposed to meet Patsy at three and it was now a quarter to.

"What's inside the base of that penguin?" he asked, still not liking the idea of just sitting in the car and waiting for whoever might show up.

"Just the stairs leading up to the slide," she replied.

He could see vents cut into the sides of the structure, vents that would give him a view of who pulled into the parking area. The woods just behind the gigantic penguin would provide cover and a possible escape route if they had to make a run for it.

If Patsy inadvertently brought the police with her and he and Caylee stayed in the car then there would be no chance for escape. "I think it would be better if we waited in there." He pointed to the penguin.

"Okay," she agreed and together they got out of the car. Her eyes widened as she saw that Micah had drawn his gun, but she said nothing.

The air was hot and soupy with humidity as they hurried across the playground to the smiling penguin. Wood chips crunched and shifted beneath their feet as Micah's gaze shot from left to right, assessing the situation for potential danger.

He breathed a sigh of relief as they reached the enclosure of the base of the slide. Just as he'd predicted, the ventilation slits provided a perfect view of the parking lot. He'd be able to see any cars that arrived.

Caylee sat on the bottom step of the slide, her slender legs tucked awkwardly beneath her. He'd awakened that morning irritated with her...with himself. Making love with her had been amazing, but what disturbed him was the aftermath when he'd gotten back into bed with her and she'd cuddled against him like she belonged in the curve of his body.

He'd lain there with her warmth pressed against him and her hair tickling the underside of his jaw, and for a brief vulnerable moment he'd wanted more than he had in his life. He wanted people in his life who would miss him, an Aunt Patsy or a cousin Rick, people whose love for him he'd never have to question.

For that brief moment he'd wanted to be part of something bigger than himself. He glanced over at Caylee who was looking down at her feet as if all the answers they sought were in her sandals.

She was so open, didn't seem to possess the internal walls that built his life, that made his choices. There was an innate goodness that drew him to her, made him want to see the world through her eyes.

"She's late," he said as he glanced at his watch. It was two minutes after three.

"She's always late," Caylee replied. "My dad used to say that when it came time to bury Aunt Patsy, the funeral home would have to schedule an extra half an hour just to wait for her to arrive."

He glanced back out of the vent. He'd feel better when this was over and done with, when they were back at the house and Caylee had her day planner in front of her. He hoped that day planner was worth this risk, that she'd flip open a page, see a name and have a Perry Mason moment.

Each day that passed without them having a lead to follow up on only increased his feeling that this was all going to eventually end badly.

A rumble of thunder sounded in the distance and only added to his feeling of approaching doom. He tightened his grip on the butt of his gun, hoping he wouldn't have to use it.

"Are you all right?" Caylee asked.

"Yeah, why?" He glanced at her once again.

She smiled, one of those soft smiles of hers that shot an instant burst of heat through his veins. "Just wondering. You know, a park…a rainy day…" She let her voice trail off and her smile was replaced by a tiny frown of concern.

He realized she was worried about him because of his past, because of the day his mother had left him sitting in the park bench in the rain. It irritated him, first that he had told her, and second, that with everything she was facing at the moment, she was worried about him.

"I said I'm fine," he exclaimed. "You think I might

go postal from some kind of post-traumatic stress thing? What happened to me as a child happened a long time ago. I dealt with it and it's over." He felt like she was getting too deep in his head, forcing him to feel things he didn't want to feel.

"You just seem tense," she replied.

"I'm tense because we're sitting in a giant penguin waiting for a woman I don't trust, wondering if she's bringing the cops."

"She wouldn't do that," Caylee replied with all the certainty in the world.

He turned back around to look out the vent once again and saw a gold-tone sedan pulling into the lot. "Does she drive a gold car?"

"Yes, yes she does." Caylee got up and came to stand just beside him. "She's alone, right?"

Micah watched the road to see if any other cars pulled off or looked suspicious. "Yeah, it looks like she's alone," he finally said. Out of the corner of his eye he saw Caylee move.

"Caylee, wait!" he cried, but it was too late. She was already out the opening of the penguin and running around the structure to meet her aunt.

He looked back through the vent to see a plump, dark-haired woman getting out of the car. She waved something in the air as Caylee came into his view, running across the wood chips toward Patsy.

She was halfway there when the unmistakeable sound of a gunshot rang in the air. Caylee hit the ground like a deer felled by a hunter's rifle. Patsy screamed and ran back toward her car as Micah exploded from the back of the penguin in a crouch.

An unexpected surge of grief welled up inside him, but he consciously shoved it aside, his gaze focused on the wooded area where he thought the shot had come from.

Let her be okay. Let her be okay. It was a constant mantra whirling around in his head as he scanned the area with narrowed eyes. He wanted to run to her, knew that if she'd been hit she'd need medical attention. But he also knew that if he ran to her and got shot, there would be nobody to help her if she was still alive.

The first rule of survival was to take care of yourself, then see to the fallen. But it was difficult to adhere to that particular rule when the fallen was Caylee.

Nothing in the woods appeared to signal danger and his instincts told him that whoever had pulled the trigger was long gone. He straightened from his crouch, half-expecting another shot to split the air, but nothing happened. Just to be on the safe side, he fired two shots into the woods.

Still in a defensive posture, he ran around the side of the giant slide and saw that Caylee still lay unmoving on the ground and Patsy's car was gone.

Heart hammering painfully fast in his chest, he rushed to Caylee. He crouched down beside her, an unexpected wealth of emotion clogging his throat. "Caylee," he finally managed to gasp.

"Is it safe?"

The strength of her voice sent a rush of relief through him. "Are you hurt?" He kept his attention divided between her and the stand of trees in the distance.

"No. I figure when somebody shoots at you and you can't get away the next best thing is to play dead." She sat up, and he moved himself in position between her and the woods.

"We need to get out of here," he said. Now that he knew she was all right, a new urgency filled him. He didn't know if Patsy would call the police. He didn't know if somebody else had heard the gunfire and dialed 911. Hell, he couldn't even be sure that the shooter was gone.

"I want you to get up real slow and then run like hell to the car," he told her. "I'll cover you from here."

Thank God she didn't take time to give him a monologue on how she liked to run or mention that it was going to rain. She simply got to her feet and took off like a bat out of hell toward their car.

Micah followed, wondering how he was going to convince Caylee that he suspected her Aunt Patsy had betrayed her trust.

Chapter Eight

Caylee had never run so fast in her life, nor had she ever
been so frightened as she'd been when she'd heard that
gunshot and instinctively dove to the ground.

Somebody had tried to kill her. There was no am-
biguity, no possibility of mistake. She'd run out from
the cover of the penguin and somebody had fired a
gun at her with the intent to kill her.

She nearly sobbed with relief as she reached the
car. She was about to get in when she spied her day
planner on the ground. Aunt Patsy must have dropped
it when she'd run back to her car.

Caylee scooped it up and then got into the car, her
limbs shaking like wind-tossed leaves on the distant
trees. The shaking didn't stop until Micah was in the
car and they were driving away from the park.

He didn't speak, and she found his silence stifling.
It only added to the terror that held her tightly in its
grip. Somebody had tried to kill her. The alien words

rocketed around and around in her head, dizzying her with their menace.

That meant that Jason's death had probably been a mistake, that somebody had been after her and had accidentally killed him instead. There was no question now that this was about her.

She noticed that Micah kept his gaze directed between the street before them and his rearview mirror, obviously looking to see if they were being followed. He kept his speed just under the limit although she knew he probably couldn't wait to get back to the safety of the house.

"At least I got my day planner," she said, not able to stand the silence a minute longer. "Aunt Patsy must have dropped it when she got back into her car."

He was silent for a long moment, his jaw muscle in a knot and throbbing like an erratic heartbeat. "She didn't even wait around to see if you were dead or alive."

An edge of hurt inched through her as she realized he was right. "I'm sure she was terrified," she said in an attempt to explain Patsy's quick escape not just to him, but also to herself. "If I had been in her shoes, I probably would have run first and asked questions later."

"Whoever shot at you was waiting for us."

Although he didn't actually say the words, the implication was clear. It had been a setup. And if that were true then she had to face the fact that her Aunt Patsy was part of it.

Her heart rebelled at the very idea even as she felt the press of hot tears behind her eyes. She was grateful that Micah said nothing else for the remainder of the drive back to the house. She couldn't bear for him to say what he had to be thinking, that somehow her aunt was responsible for the shot in the park.

When they reached the house she went directly to her bedroom and closed the door, needing time to process, wanting to be alone with the terrifying thoughts that now tried to take hold in her mind.

She was thankful when Micah didn't follow her. She threw herself on the bed and allowed her tears to fall. Her world had fallen apart and suddenly she wasn't sure who to trust.

Although her heart wanted to believe that Patsy was innocent, her head no longer had the luxury of blind belief. Had Patsy lingered at her car allowing Caylee to run the distance between them and make herself an easy target?

Had she known that somebody was hiding in the woods, waiting to take a lethal shot at her? Had she hired somebody to follow Caylee to Fortuna and wait for the right moment?

There was no question now that Jason had simply been in the wrong bed. Whoever had crept into that room and stabbed him had thought they were killing her.

Even though she'd known she was in trouble before this moment, she'd been functioning under the impression that it was all just a terrible mistake and as soon as the mistake got fixed, everything would be all right. But now, the safe world that she'd always known was gone, exploded in the crack of gunfire.

"Caylee." Micah knocked softly on her bedroom door.

"Go away. I don't want to talk right now." There was no sniffing back the tears that fell fast and furious down her cheeks.

"We need to talk," Micah called through the door. "I'm coming in." She buried her head in her arms as the bed next to her depressed with his weight.

For a long moment he didn't speak. He just sat next to her as she continued to cry. Finally he placed a hand on her shoulder. "We need to talk about what happened."

She rolled over on her back and sat up, not looking at him but rather staring across the room at the wall. "I don't want to talk about it. I don't even want to think about it."

"I know. I know, but we have to," he replied softly. "Either your Aunt Patsy told somebody she was meeting us or…"

"Or she set me up," Caylee said flatly. She squeezed her eyes tightly closed and drew a tremulous breath. When she opened her eyes again, she gazed at him, her heart aching like it had never ached before.

"You know what scares me?" she asked. He shook his head and she continued. "When this is all over, I'll be just like you, all closed off from people and all alone. I don't think I want to live in your world."

She'd half-expected her words to make him angry, but he didn't even blink. "Caylee, if your aunt didn't tell anyone she was meeting us, then we need to figure out why she might want you dead."

"I need to call her and see if she told anyone. There's got to be a logical explanation for this."

His gaze bore into hers with a piercing intensity. "What you need to do is think about why she'd want to kill you. In any case, what makes you think she'll tell you the truth if she's guilty?"

Caylee raised a hand to her temple, where a headache had begun to pound. Once again she closed her eyes, a sick knot weighing heavy in her chest. "She's my beneficiary." The words squeezed out of her constricted throat.

"Why didn't you mention this before?"

She looked at him again. "Because I didn't think it mattered before. Because nobody had shot at me before." She dropped her hand from her temple to her lap, overwhelmed by the emotions that battled inside her.

"I feel like I'm trapped in the worst nightmare I've ever had," she said.

He touched her shoulder, a light caress that she

knew was unnatural for him. "If it's any consolation, you aren't in the nightmare all alone."

She smiled, surprised that it did help, knowing that he was going to help her navigate the uncharted hot waters she found herself in.

"The first thing we need to do is find out if your aunt told anyone she was meeting us at the park." He got up from the bed and held out a hand to her.

She grasped his hand, feeling as if it were a lifeline and together they went into the living room where she picked up the cell phone she'd used to call her aunt the day before.

Her fingers trembled as she punched in the familiar number. Did the person who she thought had loved her like a mother want her dead? Was this somehow about money? Had Patsy festered with rage when Caylee's father had left the store to Caylee and not to the sister who'd helped him raise his child?

Patsy had never shown a bit of interest in the store. Even six months ago when a big chain had tried to buy the place, Patsy had encouraged Caylee not to sell.

She looked at Micah as the phone began to ring. Rick answered. "Caylee, thank God," he said. "Are you all right? Mom has been frantic. She said she tried to meet with you and somebody shot at you."

"I'm fine." She squeezed the phone tightly, fighting against a new wave of tears.

"She didn't know if you were dead or alive, but she was terrified the gunman would shoot her."

"Did she call the police?" Caylee asked.

"No, she was afraid they'd get there and arrest you. Or that they might arrest her for meeting with you."

"Rick, I need to know who Aunt Patsy might have told that she was meeting me. It's important, Rick." She gripped the receiver tight against her ear, a mental picture of her cousin filling her head.

"Hang on, let me ask her."

Caylee gripped the phone so hard her fingers grew numb. Rick came back on the line. "She said she told Vicki from the store."

Caylee frowned. "Vicki?" Her store manager would have nothing to gain by Caylee's death.

"Caylee, are you there?"

"Yes, yes I'm here."

"What can we do to help?" he asked. "The police have been here and talked to us. We told them there was no way you had anything to do with Jason's death, but I don't think they believed us. Where are you? Are you safe?"

"I'm safe," she replied. "I'm with Micah. We're just trying to figure this all out."

"Where? How can we get hold of you? Caylee, you're in bad trouble. Isn't there something we can do to help?"

"No, there's nothing you can do. I'm safe where I'm at for now." She looked at Micah. Yes, she was as safe as she could get in this world with him standing next to her. "I'll be in touch." She ended the call amid Rick's protests.

Micah looked at her expectantly. "She told Vicki, my store manager," she said.

He frowned thoughtfully and motioned her into the kitchen and to the table. He waited until she'd sat, then joined her. "Why would Vicki want you dead?"

"She wouldn't," she protested. "I mean, we've had our issues, but nothing that would make her want to kill me."

"What kind of issues?"

Once again her head pounded with nauseating intensity. "Sometimes she forgot who was boss and I had to take her down a notch. She had her own ideas of how the business should be run and they didn't always coincide with mine. But she has nothing to gain by my death. The store doesn't become hers if I die."

Before she could say anything else, Troy called from the front door. He and Luke came into the kitchen, both clad in somber suits.

"The funeral was a zoo," Luke said as he sat at the table. "There must have been five hundred people there. It looked like most of the attendees were Grant's friends and associates."

"And nobody specific sent up red flags," Troy added as he leaned a slim hip against the counter.

"That's all right. We've pretty well decided that

somebody wants Caylee dead," Micah replied. He quickly filled in his partners on the afternoon's events.

As he talked, Caylee leaned back in the chair, weary defeat making her want to just go to bed and pull the covers over her head. She wanted to cry again. Somehow she knew the comforting innocence she'd once possessed had been stolen from her.

MICAH FELT HER depression as he tried to stay focused on the conversation with Troy and Luke. "What's Vicki's last name?" he asked.

"Michaels. Vicki Michaels," she replied.

"You got an address on her?" Luke asked.

Caylee nodded. "She lives at 244 North Cambridge, apartment three."

"And you can't think of any reason why she'd want to harm you?" Troy asked as he sat down at the table.

Caylee looked at him with hollow eyes. "The only thing I can think of is that when the Berkoff Company made an offer to buy my store, she got excited about the deal. When I refused to sell she pouted for a couple of days. But that was six months ago, and it doesn't exactly seem like a good motive for murder." She stood and rubbed her temple with two fingers. "If you all will excuse me, I need to lie down for a little while."

Nobody said anything until she'd left the room. "Is she going to be all right?" Troy asked once she was gone.

"It's been a tough day for her, but she'll be fine," Micah replied. He'd been around Caylee long enough to know that she was resilient. "She's much tougher than she looks."

"You think her aunt is behind this?" Luke asked.

"I'm not sure what to believe," Micah confessed. "But, I'd like you to check into Patsy as well as this Vicki and see what you can dig up. I also want a full check into Caylee. Maybe there's something there she hasn't considered or doesn't remember." Or wasn't telling him, although he couldn't really imagine that was the case.

"Done," Troy said as he dug into his suit jacket pocket. He pulled out several sheets of neatly folded paper and pushed them across the table toward Micah. "These are the passenger lists of all commercial flights from Lake Charles to Kansas City on the night of the murder."

Lake Charles was the city everyone flew into to catch the ferry to Fortuna. Whoever had killed Jason would have had to catch a flight from the Lake Charles airport that night in order to get the knife into Caylee's apartment the next day.

"What about private flight information?" Micah asked.

"Still working on it," Troy replied.

"None of the names of anyone we've talked about is on those lists," Luke said. "But maybe Caylee will recognize a name."

"You know we could probably get you out of this mess," Troy said in a low voice. "You had a reason to be in Fortuna, and between the time you got off the ferry and the time you were in the air, there wasn't really opportunity for you to kill Jason."

"Even Kincaid can't make the hard evidence go away," Luke added. "There's no way you'd be found guilty. And we have the resources to keep you out of jail on bail."

It could be over. He could get out of this house and on with his life. For just a moment he wanted to embrace the idea. He wanted his own bed, the solitude of his own thoughts. But even as he entertained the thought, a vision of soft green eyes came to mind, the scent of Caylee eddied in his head.

"I'm not bailing on her," he replied. "She's in trouble and needs my help. She has no idea how to navigate her way through this mess and there's no question that her life is in danger. I can't just walk away from her."

Troy nodded. "Just wanted to make sure we were all on the same page." He got up. "We'll be back tomorrow and have information for you on the people you mentioned."

Micah walked them to the front door, then went back to the living room and sank down on the sofa. He should take the list of names that Troy had left in to Caylee and make her look at them, but he decided to leave her alone.

It had been obvious that she had a headache. And the day's events had been traumatic enough. She deserved to be left alone for a while.

He could only assume that Patsy hadn't called the police after the shooting in the park to save her own ass. Was it because she'd been part of the plot to harm Caylee? The fact that she hadn't called the authorities only added to his suspicion of the woman.

He eyed the cell phone on the coffee table. He reached out and picked it up. A glance at his watch let him know it was almost six. He didn't know if Chief Kincaid would be working late or not, but it was time to make contact.

He punched in the number of the downtown police department, knowing it by heart. Before making a repossession in the city, they usually gave a heads up to the local police department as a courtesy.

"Chief Kincaid, please. Tell him Micah Stone is on the line." He clutched the phone tightly against his ear, preparing himself for the voice of his nemesis.

It was a moment before he got on the phone. "Stone, a fine mess you've gotten yourself into," Kincaid said, his deep voice booming across the line. "Where are you?"

Micah released a dry laugh. "Do you really expect me to answer that? Listen, you're after the wrong people in the Worthington death. I had nothing to do with it and neither did Caylee Warren. We both just happened to be at the wrong place at the wrong time."

"Turn yourself in and we'll talk about it," Kincaid replied.

"Unfortunately, I don't have much confidence that you'll act as an unbiased lawman," Micah replied. "I just want you to know that Jason wasn't the intended victim. Caylee and I were at Penguin Park today and somebody took a shot at her."

"Nobody reported a gunshot in that area of town today," he said with more than a touch of disbelief.

"Just because nobody reported it doesn't mean it didn't happen," Micah replied. "I'm telling you, Caylee is the one in danger, and you should be investigating that."

"Don't tell me how to do my job, you little bastard," Kincaid exploded. "You might as well turn yourself in. Because I'm going to find you. There's no place the two of you can hide where I won't eventually hunt you down."

"Find the real killer," Micah exclaimed. "Somebody is after Caylee. That's who you should be looking for."

There was a long moment of silence, and he could hear Kincaid draw a deep breath as if to steady himself. Micah took the opportunity to continue. "Wendall, don't let our personal history blind you to the truth. Whoever killed Jason Worthington was actually trying to get Caylee. Until I know she's safe, until I know you're on the same page as us, we're not coming in."

He didn't wait for a response and hung up, his frustration level through the ceiling. "Are you okay?" He whirled around at the sound of her voice.

Caylee stood in the hallway, her beautiful face radiating concern.

"Yeah, I'm all right." He tossed the phone back on the coffee table and sat heavily on the sofa. She walked over to the sofa beside him, then leaned her head on his shoulder as if it were the most natural thing in the world.

Just that easily, his tension ebbed. Maybe it was the scent of her that had become as familiar as his own heartbeat, or the warmth of her body resting so trustingly against his own, but for the moment it just felt right for them to sit silently and draw strength from each other.

"Troy brought the list of passenger names from flights in and out of Lake Charles on the night Jason was killed," he said, finally breaking the silence.

"Not now. Not tonight," she said firmly. "I don't want to even think about murder for the rest of the night. I'm physically and mentally exhausted."

He was surprised to realize that he was exhausted as well. He was accustomed to missions that had a beginning, a middle and an end and it bothered him that he couldn't see the end of this particular dilemma.

"That was Chief Kincaid that you were talking to?" she asked. He nodded. She placed a hand on his leg just above his knee. It wasn't a sexual touch but one he knew was meant to comfort. "It didn't sound like he was willing to listen to reason."

"That man wouldn't know reason if it jumped up and bit him in the ass," he retorted.

She giggled, a wonderfully girlish sound that winged its way into a dark corner of his heart. "Glad you find that amusing."

She smiled. "I think I've finally reached the slap-happy stage. Besides, the alternative to laughing is to cry and I've done enough of that over the past couple of days."

"I think you've handled yourself very well considering the circumstances," he observed.

She sighed and seemed to melt even more closely against him. "I still can't believe that anyone in my family could possibly be responsible for this. There's got to be another answer." She sat up and stared at him with her gorgeous green eyes. "Why now? What's happened that suddenly I've become expendable?"

"You aren't expendable, Caylee, and I'm going to do everything in my power to make sure that nothing happens to you." He pulled her back against him.

"I'm so glad it was you in the pilot seat of that plane." Her fingers pressed against his leg. "I don't know where I would be right now, what I'd be doing if it hadn't been for you. You believe that things happen for a reason, Micah?"

"No. I believe crap happens for no reason, and we

do the best we can with what we're given. There's no rhyme or reason for any of it," he replied.

"I don't believe that," she said. "I just haven't figured out what the reason is for this particular mess yet."

"You'll let me know when you figure it out?"

She smiled up at him. "I promise you'll be the first to know."

All of a sudden she was too close, her hand was too warm on his leg. He felt suffocated, like he couldn't breathe. He pushed her hand aside and stood. "I'm going to go see about fixing some dinner. I'll let you know when it's ready."

He breathed easier when he escaped alone into the kitchen. Alone. That's the way he was supposed to be, that's the way he was most comfortable. And he couldn't forget that.

Chapter Nine

As usual, morning found them both seated at the kitchen table. The sun drifted through the window, warming Caylee's back as she studied the list of passenger names Troy had brought the day before.

From the nearby utility room, the small washing machine churned a load of clothes, and the dryer emitted the scent of fabric softener. Under other circumstances, the morning would have felt normal, even comforting. But this wasn't normal circumstances. She was looking for the name of somebody who wanted her dead.

She took a sip of her coffee and glanced at Micah. He sat across from her, reading news stories he'd printed off the Internet that morning.

The frost was back in his eyes this morning. He'd been distant and cool after dinner and had apparently awakened in the same frame of mind. Those moments of closeness when they'd sat together on the sofa the night before seemed like a long time ago.

She sighed and looked back at the list of names. She didn't expect to see anyone she recognized. Surely whoever was after her was smart enough not to use their real name or take a commercial flight to the scene of a murder.

"Do you really expect me to find a name here?" she finally asked.

He looked up at her. "Probably not, but you never know."

She released another sigh. "I'm starting to think that the only way to prove my innocence is to end up dead. If I'm killed then maybe the police will realize I didn't murder Jason."

"Seems a bit extreme to prove a point," he observed dryly.

"Yeah, well I'm feeling a bit extreme this morning." She took another sip of her coffee and gazed out the window. In truth what she felt this morning was a simmering sense of desperation.

Life was passing by while she was cooped up in this house. She wanted to be at her store, back at her apartment. She wanted her life back. And they were no closer to attaining that goal than they'd been the night they'd arrived at this house.

"What happens if this never gets solved? Murders go unsolved all the time, and as long as the police are focused on us as suspects, they're never going to find the real killer. We can't spend the rest of our lives cooped up here, afraid to leave, afraid that eventually the police will show up on the doorstep." She paused to draw a breath, recognizing in the back of her mind that she was rambling as usual.

He blinked his cool blue eyes. "Are you through?"

"I'm not sure. Give me a minute." She dropped the list she'd been studying and leaned back in her chair. "I'm scared, Micah. I'm scared that we're never going to get our lives back."

"We'll figure it out," he replied. "After you go through those passenger lists, you need to look at your day planner and see if any name jumps out at you."

It wasn't the answer she wanted from him. She'd wanted something more definitive, his promise that her world would be returned to its normal place. But he didn't make promises. He didn't believe in promises, and she didn't know why that made her so sad. She returned her attention to the lists in front of her.

They were still seated at the table when Troy arrived. The handsome blonde poured himself a cup of coffee, then joined them at the table.

"If you've brought bad news, then just keep it to yourself," Caylee said half seriously.

"I wouldn't say I have bad news, just some illuminating facts," he replied.

"Like what?" Micah asked.

"I think you can cross off the possibility that one of Jason's ex-girlfriends is responsible. The last two women he dated got restraining orders against him after they broke up."

"I sure know how to pick them," Caylee exclaimed with a touch of disgust. "I waited five years to date a guy, and the guy I finally picked was a creep." Despite her words, a weight of guilt descended over her. Even though Jason had been a creep, he hadn't deserved what had happened to him. She couldn't help but feel partially responsible for his death.

"Bad luck," Troy said and then pointed to the list in front of her. "Have you found any familiar names?"

"No, not even vaguely familiar," she replied, unable to keep the disappointment from her voice.

"We checked out your newest employee, Marvin Bishop. On paper he looks like a stand-up guy. No criminal background. Just a speeding ticket two years ago. I don't think he's our man. We're not sure where to go from here," Troy admitted to Micah. "Unless we can come up with a viable motive or a specific suspect, we've run into a dead end."

"I still have my day planner to go through," Caylee said, refusing to admit defeat. "Maybe the answer is there." She couldn't give up the last of her hope. There had to be a way out of this for both of them.

"You didn't really make it clear just how successful your jewelry store has been," Troy said, his gray eyes focused on her.

"You checked me out? Looked into my finances?" For a split second she was irritated, but the emotion lasted only a moment. She had nothing to hide, and if digging around in her personal life helped them solve this mess, then let them dig. "I've said all along I wasn't interested in the Worthington money."

"What you didn't mention is that if you'd sold your shop to the Berkoff Company it would have netted you a cool million," Troy replied.

Micah sat up straighter in his chair. "Is that true?"

"I didn't take the offer, so what difference does it make?" she replied. "The store was never commercial property to me. It was my father's dream. I never really considered selling it no matter what the offer."

"Yeah, well I'll bet you didn't know that your manager, Vicki, has been dating the Berkoff heir, Eric."

Caylee once again sat back in her chair, stunned by this particular tidbit of news. "I knew she'd been dating a guy for some time, but she rarely talked about him." She frowned. "No wonder she was disappointed when I didn't sell the shop. Maybe she was promised the position of manager if I sold out. But that's hardly a motive for murder. For her it would have been just a job."

"People have killed for less," Micah replied, his brow wrinkled in thought. He slammed a fist down on the table. "Dammit, we shouldn't be chasing all this down, Kincaid should be doing it."

"He's not taking any calls from me or Luke," Troy said.

"I called him last night," Micah replied.

Troy raised a blond eyebrow. "And?"

"And that man wouldn't know reason if it bit him on the ass," Caylee said.

Troy offered her a small smile. "Sounds like you've been talking to Micah." His smile disappeared. "I checked into your Aunt Patsy's finances as well. She obviously lives a simple life, and I didn't see any signs of financial stress. Same with your cousin, Rick. Although his finances are a little more complicated by his business, he seems to be holding his own. Of course we just did cursory checks. We haven't had time to really dig deep."

"I told you they weren't really suspects," she exclaimed. "If you take away any kind of money angle, they have no reason to want me dead. They're my family. I've said over and over again that they would never want to hurt me."

"Do you have any idea how many deaths come at the hands of family members?" Micah asked. "Whenever there is a murder, the first suspects are always those closest to the victim."

"I realize that, but not in my family." How could she make a man like Micah understand the love, the closeness that had existed between them. Micah didn't know about family love, and he certainly didn't allow anyone to get close to him.

"There was only one thing that raised a red flag in their financial statements," Troy continued. "On the day that Jason was murdered, your aunt took out a two thousand dollar cash advance from one of her credit cards. Do you know what that's about?"

A lump formed in Caylee's throat. She knew what the two men suspected, but it simply couldn't be true. "I don't know what it might have been for, but it's not what you think." A hysterical burst of laughter rose to her lips, but she swallowed it. "Surely it costs more than two grand to have somebody killed."

"Considering how badly the job was botched, she obviously hired an amateur," Micah said darkly.

She glared at him. "This whole discussion is ridiculous," she exclaimed.

"Luke is trying to get copies of all of the evidence the police have from his buddy on the force," Troy said in an attempt to move forward. He leaned back in his chair and looked first at Caylee, then at Micah. "I think we have to face the possibility that we might not find the answers we're after, that you two might have to take a chance with the judicial system."

Caylee's heart fell to the floor at the same time Micah shook his head vehemently. "I'm not ready to do that yet. I'm not sure I'll ever be ready," he said to Troy.

He looked at Caylee and for just a moment his warm, blue eyes wrapped around the cold spots in her heart. "But, I'll understand if you want to call it quits, turn yourself in and take your chances to try to get back to your normal life."

The idea of getting back to her life was appealing,

but what was more appealing to her was seeing this thing through with Micah. Besides, the odds were good she'd be in jail instead of enjoying any kind of normal life. She reached out and covered his hand with hers. He turned his hand over, entwining his warm fingers with hers. And in that simple act she knew her decision was right.

"I'm not going anywhere," she said. "We're partners, remember? Partners until the end."

He gave her a curt nod, pulled his hand away from hers and looked at Troy. "It looks like we're in this for the long haul. Keep digging, buddy. We need somebody to dig us out of the hole we're in."

"We're trying. It's just too bad we can't get Kincaid on board. He's so focused on proving you guilty, I'm afraid he's missing important clues."

The conversation continued for another thirty minutes or so. When Troy left, and while Caylee studied her day planner, Micah paced the kitchen floor.

He was like a caged animal, and she found the tug of his shirt across his shoulders and the way his jeans fit on his lean hips far more interesting than the minutia of her boring life that her day planner held.

She wanted him again. The thought startled her. And she wanted even more of him than before. She wanted his dreams. She wanted to find a way into the heart he guarded so ferociously.

In the crazy mess of all of this she was precariously close to falling in love with Micah Stone. And that scared her more than spending the rest of her life in prison for a crime she didn't commit.

THE DAY PLANNER yielded no answers. Luke and Troy were chasing leads to nowhere, and Micah had never felt so frustrated in his entire life.

It wasn't just the fact that they couldn't identify a viable suspect. It was Caylee who had him on edge.

He would have felt better if she'd decided to turn herself in, get away from this house, get away from him. He'd feel better if she didn't smell like an exotic flower garden and smile at him with that sunny, bright smile that made him want to believe in things he'd never believed before.

He feared that she was going to be tainted by this, that her innocence would be lost. He'd love to possess her unshakable conviction that nobody who loved her was capable of this, but he didn't.

Fathers didn't step up, mothers left and an aunt could have resented taking care of a child who wasn't hers, seeing the successful family business pass her by.

They had just eaten dinner, and Caylee was curled up in her usual corner of the sofa. He didn't want to sit next to her, was afraid that she'd lean her head against him, place a hand on his leg. Any touch from her might shatter him.

Since the night they'd made love, there hadn't been a minute that had passed when he hadn't thought about repeating the act. She called to him like no other woman in his life ever had and he wanted to run from her faster than any woman he'd ever known.

"You're making me dizzy," she said, breaking the silence that had grown to mammoth proportions between them. "Why don't you sit down and relax?"

"I can't relax," he replied tersely. He raked a hand through his hair and glared at her. "This whole thing is starting to tick me off."

"And you're yelling at me because?" She arched an eyebrow.

He shoved his hands in his pockets and stared at her moodily. "Because there's nobody else to yell at."

"Then if it makes you feel better, yell away. I can take it," she replied.

"Nah, it would be kind of like kicking a puppy."

She gave him a mock look of outrage. "Are you calling me a dog?" She frowned then. "If you were a dog, I think you'd be a German shepherd or maybe a pit bull. I'd be a poodle."

"Or a Chihuahua. I hear they yap a lot," he replied.

She smiled. "You aren't going to make me mad, Micah. I've seen enough crime drama shows to know that things start to unravel when partners bicker." The laughter that bubbled out of him was a surprise. Her eyes shone brighter. "I'll tell you one thing. If I had to be on the lam with anyone, I'm glad I'm with you."

His heart pumped with desire for her. He wanted to yank off her clothes and take her right there on the sofa.

He picked up the list of people they'd come up with earlier that afternoon. A list of potential suspects. Patsy Jackson headed the list, even though Caylee insisted her aunt was innocent. Following Patsy's name was her son's, Rick. Vicki Michaels, Grant Worthington and John Raymond all held prominent positions on the list.

John Raymond's name had come from the day planner. He was a local artist who had contacted Caylee to see if she'd be interested in carrying his handmade jewelry. She hadn't been, but he'd continued to come around the store and had asked her out several times. A potential suitor who had become obsessive in his desire for her? An obsession that had turned to hate?

Micah set down the list and picked up his cell phone. He needed to move things forward and get them the hell out of this situation.

He punched in the number for the police station and walked down the hallway to his bedroom, needing to concentrate and unable to do so with Caylee in his line of vision.

By the time he reached his bedroom he had Wendall Kincaid on the phone. "You've got to listen to me, Kincaid," he said. He sat on the edge of his bed and waited for the chief to reply.

"I'm listening," he said after a long moment of silence.

"We've been doing some investigating of our

own and I think you need to be looking at the members of Caylee's family and the manager at the store she owns. They all have motives for wanting her dead. I have another name for you, too. John Raymond. He's a local artist who might have developed an unhealthy obsession with Caylee. It was never about Jason Worthington. Caylee is the key to all of this."

"Then bring her in," Kincaid said, his deep voice weary. "Let us talk to her."

"And you won't arrest her?"

"You know I can't promise you that," Kincaid exclaimed, the weariness gone and an edge of anger deepening his voice. "Dammit, Micah, you're only making things worse for yourself and Ms. Warren. Turn yourselves in before it's too late."

"Let me ask you a question, Kincaid. If I hadn't slept with your sister, would there be a warrant out for my arrest right now?" That night of bad judgment and too much alcohol seemed like a lifetime ago.

"Don't be ridiculous. This has nothing to do with you and my sister," Kincaid protested. "This has to do with evidence."

"You can't have anything tying me or Caylee to the murder. We didn't do it," Micah exclaimed. "I don't know which district attorney issued our arrest warrants without any real evidence, but I can tell you this, even a half-asleep defense attorney will rip this case apart and leave you with egg on your face."

"If that's what you believe, then turn yourself in," Kincaid replied.

"I'd do that if I was sure I wouldn't get a bullet in the back the first time I turned it to you. Or that one of your goons won't beat the hell out of me just because it would make you feel better."

"I guess you'd just have to take that chance," Kincaid replied.

"For God's sake, Wendall, just do your job. Find out who wants Caylee Warren dead. That's the person who murdered Jason Worthington. She's in danger and you aren't helping things by being so damned bull-headed." Micah hung up, aware that he'd accomplished nothing with the call.

He tossed the phone on the bed and raked his hand through his hair once again. He was reluctant to join Caylee in the living room, but even more reluctant to be alone with his own thoughts.

Hopelessness was an emotion he rarely allowed himself to feel. Even on the missions that had looked futile, when he and his SEAL buddies had thought death was imminent, he'd never lost hope. But at this moment, as he stood in the center of the bedroom, hopelessness nearly overwhelmed him.

He returned to the living room where Caylee offered him a soft smile and patted the sofa next to her. "Come sit, Micah. There's nothing more we can do tonight."

The last thing he should do was sit close to her,

and yet it was the thing he wanted most. As if his feet had a mind of their own, he walked across the room and sank into the cushion next to her.

Instantly the scent of her engulfed him. But it was the quiet calm that emanated from her that he relished. Although they didn't touch, the heat of her body warmed him, and once again a buck of desire for her kicked him midsection.

"No matter how much evidence Troy and Luke dig up on my Aunt Patsy and Rick, I'll never believe that either of them are behind this," she said softly. "We were always a close family, and the bond only got stronger when my father passed away. You can't fake that kind of love."

"I wouldn't know about that," he replied.

"I've been thinking about that." She shifted positions so she was facing him, her features soft with reflective thought.

"Thinking about what?"

"About you and about your mother."

A new tension filled him, momentarily squashing the rise of desire he'd felt. "What about her?"

"Have you ever thought that maybe it was her love for you that caused her to leave you on that park bench?" He stared at her, the words not making sense in his brain. His mother hadn't dropped him off with friends or put him up for adoption. She'd abandoned him on a park bench in the rain. "You said your life with her wasn't so great," she continued. "Maybe she wanted to give you more, maybe it was the ultimate sacrifice of love. A hope that you'd have a better life than what she could provide for you."

The emotion that burned up the back of his throat was one he'd never allowed himself to feel before. For a moment he couldn't draw a breath, felt as if he were suffocating. He was that frightened little boy sitting in the rain, held there by his mother's promise.

Anger swept in and he embraced it. He jumped up from the sofa. "Maybe you'd better mind your own business, and think about how in the hell we're going to get out of this mess."

Her eyes narrowed. "Well, excuse me for trying to help. I won't make that mistake again."

"Good, then we're clear." Anger still swelled inside him.

"You're an ass," she exclaimed.

He picked up the car keys from the coffee table. "I'm going out. I'll be back later."

She stumbled to her feet, a worried frown tugging her forehead. "Wait, Micah. Where are you going?"

He hesitated at the door. *Away from you, away from all the things you make me feel.* The words filled his head but didn't cross his lips. "I just need some space. Go to bed, Caylee. I'll see you in the morning."

He didn't wait for her reply, stepping out into the muggy night.

Chapter Ten

She'd upset him. Caylee flopped back down on the sofa and stared unseeing at the television. It certainly hadn't been her intention to make him mad. She'd only wanted to give him some peace.

She should have known better than to stick her nose in his business. He'd obviously done just fine in life without her interference. Except there were moments when she felt his loneliness and wanted to fill all the empty spaces inside him.

As crazy as it sounded, in the brief time she'd known him, in the days they'd spent together in this old farmhouse, she'd fallen in love with Micah Stone.

Wrapping her arms around herself, she leaned back into the cushions and considered the depth of her feelings for him. Were they merely a product of the situation? Would she be feeling this way about any man that shared this house, this mess with her?

The answer came to her in a single word. No. She hadn't fallen for Micah simply because he was convenient and they shared the same living space. She loved the sound of his laughter, liked the quiet confidence that emanated from him.

She didn't know what forces made people fall in love, she only knew that something about Micah caused a hitch in her breathing, a warmth in her heart that she'd never felt for another man. It was more than just desire. It went deeper than that.

And she'd driven him right out of the house. She shook her head ruefully and used the remote to turn off the television. The sudden silence of the house was deafening.

Her mind began to race with the memory of the conversation they'd had with Troy earlier that day. Why would her aunt have taken out a two thousand dollar advance on a credit card? Although there was no way she would ever believe that it had been used as some sort of down payment to a hit man, she couldn't imagine what the money had been for.

What she wanted to do more than anything was call Patsy and talk to her, but she knew Micah would be upset with her if she did. And he was already upset enough.

She picked up the list of suspects she'd written up early in the afternoon. Staring at the names she tried to figure out who might want her dead. A headache began to pound at her temples.

The fact that two of the people on the list were family members broke her heart. But she had to look at Patsy and Rick as potential suspects. Had Vicki arranged for her death in an effort to gain control of the jewelry store? She thought of the pretty, dark-haired young woman whom she'd butted heads with on more than one occasion.

When this was all over, she'd fire Vicki. She should have done it months ago, but the fact that she didn't trust her own manager told her it was time for a change no matter what.

She stared at John Raymond's name. She'd forgotten about the quirky artist until she'd looked over her day planner. He'd asked her out several times before she'd left for Fortuna with Jason, but she'd declined his invitations for a date.

Had his pleasant features hidden a whacked-out mind? Had he gone to Fortuna to murder her because she'd rejected his advances? She'd certainly seen news stories about men who stalked women and committed murders because of unrequited love, but she'd never imagined something like that would happen to her.

She remained on the sofa until almost ten o'clock, then decided to do what Micah had told her to and call it a night. He'd made it clear that he might be gone awhile.

As she left the living room and went down the hallway to her bedroom she wondered where he had gone, what he was doing. She hoped he wasn't doing anything that might put him in danger. The last thing she wanted was for him to be arrested by Kincaid.

She changed into her nightgown and got into bed thinking it would be hours before she could shut down her mind enough to find sleep. But she was wrong. Sleep came almost immediately and with it dreams.

She dreamed of Micah's laughter and the warmth his blue eyes could contain, warmth that seeped right into her heart. She dreamed of him crawling into bed with her, wrapping her up in his big strong arms and holding her tight against his chest.

The pleasant dream transformed and Micah disappeared. Instead she saw her Aunt Patsy in the back of a car, paying off a man who looked like he'd jumped off a wanted poster. "Kill her," Patsy said, her usual warm brown eyes icy with hate. "I raised her as a favor to my brother and when he died he left everything to her. Didn't leave me anything after all I'd done for him."

She stirred, barely surfacing into consciousness as the dream faded. A noise sounded. The faint hiss of a window rising? Even though she knew she was still more than half asleep, her heart began to beat a little quicker, but she couldn't quite get awake.

Warm muggy night air caressed her face at the same time the edge of the bed depressed with weight. The last moments of sleep ebbed away. "Micah?"

She began to sit up, but was pushed back down with such force, the back of her head cracked against the wooden headboard. Nauseating pain shot through her head as stars momentarily danced in front of her eyes.

Before she could recover, a heavy body straddled hers, and strong hands encased in plastic gloves encircled her neck.

Get up! a panicked voice screamed in her mind. It had to be a dream…a nightmare. All she had to do was wake up and everything would be fine.

As the hands began to squeeze and the pain in the back of her head intensified, she knew it wasn't a dream, it was horrifying reality.

She bucked in an attempt to throw her attacker off her, but he remained firmly on top. She grabbed his wrists and pulled, wanting, needing them off her throat. She tried to scream but it came out as a strained whimper quickly choked off by the strength of his hands.

Frantically she thrashed, tears seeping from her eyes as she fought for her life. Even as she struggled to fight him off, her mind raced with the need to identify him, but the room was too dark to see his face.

Micah, where are you? She cried his name over and over again in her mind as the man's hands squeezed tighter and the darkness of the room began to seep into her head.

She was going to die. And she'd never known why…would never know who was responsible. With a final burst of desperation, she reached up and grabbed his hair, hoping that when Micah found her dead she would at least have a handful of DNA evidence. With all her remaining strength she yanked.

He hissed and his hands momentarily loosened. "Bitch," he spat, his breath warm on her face.

From the living room she heard the sound of the front door squeaking open, felt a shift in the air.

Her attacker froze for an instant, then jumped off her and dove for the open window. Caylee gulped air, then released a scream that ripped the insides of her throat and had enough power to raise the dead.

Her bedroom door exploded inward and the light overhead blinked on, momentarily blinding her. When she focused she saw Micah with gun in hand and eyes narrowed and dangerous.

She didn't need to tell him what had happened. He crossed the room like a stalking animal and slid out of the window as silently as a shadow.

Caylee sat up, a sob escaping from her aching throat. That first sob was followed by another, and then another as she realized how very close she'd come to death.

She brought her knees up to her chest and wrapped her arms around them, a swell of emotion making it impossible for her to do anything else.

As she cried, she kept her gaze focused on the window, willing Micah to return. Minutes passed in a haze of pain. Her head pounded and her throat burned each time she swallowed.

Another minute and she'd have been unconscious. A few minutes after that and she would have been dead. If Micah hadn't returned when he had, he would have found her cold, lifeless body in the morning.

Micah appeared at the window, his face without expression, his eyes flat and cold as a reptile. "Get dressed and get your things together. We've got to get out of here."

He crawled through the window and slammed it shut. She stared at him as the attack replayed in her mind. She'd been so close to death. An icy fist clenched around her heart.

"Caylee, get up. Get moving. We've been compromised. We've got to leave." He walked over to the bed, grabbed her by the hands and muscled her to a standing position. "I'm driving away from here in about three minutes. Either pull it together and get your stuff or I swear I'll leave you here."

His words penetrated through her horror. She'd just been brutally attacked and now he was yelling at her and threatening to leave her. White-hot anger ripped through her. She wanted to slap his face, kick him for being an insensitive ass. Before she got the chance, he released her hands and left the bedroom.

She heard him moving quickly in his room, and knowing he was gathering his personal items, she did the same. As she threw everything into the duffel bag that Luke had provided, she realized Micah had made her angry for her own good, to get her past the shock, past the trauma so she'd move.

There would be time later to process what had happened, to explore each and every moment of the attack. But right now the important thing was for them to get out of here before anything else happened.

She met him in the hallway, heart pumping and head pounding. He gave her a curt nod, then led the way to the front door. When they reached the door he once again pulled his gun. "When I step out on the porch, you run for the car and get inside," he said. "Ready?"

She nodded and tightened her grip on the duffel bag handle. As he stepped outside, gun raised and ready, she swept past him and ran for the car.

She didn't breathe easier until they were both safely in the car, pulling away from the house. It was after midnight, and the darkness of the night was profound, without the benefit of even a sliver of moon showing through the clouds.

"Where are we going?" she asked.

His features looked harsh and strained in the illumination from the dash. "We'll find a cheap motel to hole up in." He shifted his hands on the steering wheel. "Did you see who it was?"

"No, it was too dark." She didn't want to talk about it, didn't even want to think about it until they were someplace safe. Thankfully he didn't ask her any more questions.

She tried to ignore the headache that roared through the back of her head, but it was all she could think of. That, and the fact that death had blown its hot breath on her face.

They traveled for about twenty minutes, him dividing his attention between the road ahead and his rearview mirror. Then he pulled into the parking lot of the Lazy Owl Motel.

The blinking Vacancy sign had a dozen burned-out bulbs, and the only other vehicle in the parking lot was a rusty pickup truck.

"It's not exactly a five-star hotel," he said as he pulled up in front of the office. "Hell, it's not even a one-star, but it's a place where cash serves as identification and nobody asks questions. You wait here. I'll be back in a minute."

"Wait!" She reached over and clutched his arm in desperation. "Maybe I should come in, too." She didn't want to be left alone for a minute.

"Caylee." For the first time since the endless night had begun his voice was soft, his gaze warm as he looked at her. "You aren't exactly dressed to go inside the office with me."

She stared down at the short, scarlet silk nightgown. The last thing on her mind had been her attire when he'd told her they were leaving the house in three minutes. She'd stepped into her flip-flops and then had packed. She released her hold on his arm.

"You'll be fine," he said. "We weren't followed and nobody knows we're here. Lock the door and I'll be out in a minute or two." She fought against rising panic as he left the car. She quickly pushed the button that locked all four doors.

She looked around, afraid of the shadows, afraid of what the night might hide. Her fingers touched her neck and she winced as she felt the welts that were physical proof of what she'd just been through.

True to his word Micah returned to the car within minutes. He slid back behind the steering wheel and handed her a key sporting a large plastic tab that read 108.

"I paid for a week," he said as he pulled up in front of the unit that matched the room number on the key tab. "Cash. Nobody will know we're here unless we tell them."

They grabbed their duffel bags and got out of the car. Despite the lateness of the hour the scent of grease and French fries rode the air from a nearby fast food place. At least they wouldn't starve.

The adrenaline rush that had carried her since the attack had evaporated, and she was suddenly more weary than she'd ever been in her life.

He opened the door to reveal two double beds covered in the requisite gold nappy spreads. A scarred nightstand stood between the beds, an ugly brass lamp bolted to the wood.

The room smelled of staleness and cheap pine cleaner, but Caylee didn't care. It was safe…they were safe, at least for now, and that was all she cared about.

She dropped her duffel bag on the nearest bed and Micah promptly placed it on the other bed. "I sleep next to the door," he said. He dropped his bag, sat on the bed and patted the space next to him. "Now, tell me exactly what happened."

Emotion swelled up in her chest and her vision misted with the press of hot tears. She realized she wasn't crying because of the attack, but rather because they were on a downward spiral. The end was rushing toward them like a speeding locomotive and they were trapped smack dab in the middle of the tracks.

SINCE THE MOMENT Micah had burst into her bedroom and saw the open window, the red and purple bruising of her neck and the sheer terror in her eyes, he hadn't allowed himself to feel.

But as she sank next to him and he wrapped his arm around her slender, shaking shoulders, raw emotion clawed at him. If he'd stayed in the bar for one more beer, he would have found her dead body. If he'd been held up by a stoplight or lingered in his car before going inside the house, the assailant would have strangled her to death.

He squeezed her tightly against his side, horrified by how close he'd come to losing her. He wished he could get his hands on whoever had crawled into that window, the man who had made the marks on her neck. He would have truly been wanted for murder if he'd managed to catch the guy.

She finally stopped crying long enough to tell him what had happened.

His heart shuddered as he thought of her alone and

vulnerable. It was his fault. He should have never left the house. He'd allowed a comment about his mother to get under his skin, a comment Caylee had meant to comfort him. And she'd almost paid with her life.

She now looked up at him, and her eyes held an expression that would haunt him for the rest of his life. "I thought I was going to die."

"It's all right. You're safe now," he replied. "You said it was too dark to see him. Did he say anything to you?"

"Not at first. I pulled his hair. I figured if he killed me at least I'd have a handful of his hair in my fingers and you could do a DNA test or whatever and find out who killed me. When I yanked on his hair he called me a bitch. I...I smelled his breath." She froze and her entire body tensed as she released a small gasp.

"What? What is it?"

She gazed up at him, her eyes hollow and lifeless in a way he'd never seen before. "Spearmint." She said the word as if it explained everything. "His breath smelled like spearmint." Her eyes filled with tears and she shook her head from side to side as if to deny whatever she was thinking.

He looked at her in confusion. "Caylee, why are you crying? What are you thinking?"

"A year ago, my cousin Rick quit smoking and started chewing spearmint gum. But lots of people chew gum, right? That doesn't mean it was Rick. It could have been somebody else. It was probably somebody else." Her smile was brittle, threatening to shatter into a million pieces as she gazed at him, willing him to agree with her, but his blood ran cold with the information.

He'd always feared deep in his heart that the guilty person was somebody close to her, somebody she cared about, and even though he couldn't imagine the why of it, he knew instinctively she'd identified the who.

She must have seen it in his eyes, for she seemed to grow smaller in his arms, and she began to tremble once again. "It can't be him," she protested, although her voice was weak and reedy. "It doesn't make sense. It just doesn't make sense."

It was the moment he'd feared would come, when the sweet innocence she possessed would be blown apart and she would never be the same again.

"Maybe it was somebody else," he heard himself saying, knowing he was probably giving her false hope, but unable to stop himself. "We'll check him out."

"I thought he'd already been checked out," she replied. "Troy looked into his finances."

Micah nodded. "There's been so many suspects that Troy and Luke have only done cursory checks on the people involved. Now it's time for them to dig deeper into Rick's life and see what they turn up. Maybe he has a solid alibi for the time of the attack, an alibi that will leave no question as to his innocence."

She released a deep sigh. "I can't imagine why he'd want to hurt me. He isn't my beneficiary, and we've never exchanged a cross word. I've been like his big sister. When we were young, I helped him study for tests and I made him cream cheese and jelly sandwiches whenever he wanted. When he got older, I encouraged him to open his own business and was always there for him when he needed advice."

She was rambling, but he didn't mind. That was the way she processed things, by talking through it all out loud. As she talked, his mind raced.

What motive could Rick have for wanting Caylee dead? Even though he knew sometimes motives were murky and hard to discern, there was always a reason for murder.

Was it possible Rick resented having to share his mother for all those years? Had Patsy shoved her own son aside to embrace Caylee as the daughter she'd never had? Was it a case of a sick, twisted sibling rivalry taken to the extreme?

He suddenly realized Caylee had stopped talking and was leaning more heavily against him. "Let's get some sleep," he said. "It's late and we can figure this all out in the morning."

She looked up at him, tears clinging to her long dark lashes. "I've always believed that at the end of the day, all a person really has is the love of their friends and family. If Rick did this then I'll have nothing to hang on to, nothing to believe in."

He wanted to tell her that she could believe in him, that she could hang on to him as long as she needed, as long as she wanted. But it felt like a promise and he didn't want the heat and emotion of the moment to make him say something he would later regret.

"Go to bed, Caylee. You'll feel better in the morning."

She stirred from his arms and stood. He tried not to notice how the short silky nightgown displayed the length of her perfectly shaped legs and barely covered the full thrust of her breasts.

She didn't say another word as she pulled down the bedspread on her bed and crawled beneath the sheets. Micah waited until she closed her eyes, then he took off his shoes and socks, pulled his shirt off over his head and shucked his jeans. He got into the other bed and reached over to turn out the light.

Through the curtains at the window, the blinking red vacancy sign was visible. The bed was lumpy and he had a feeling sleep would be a long time coming.

How had Rick found them? He must have managed to tail Troy or Luke when they'd come to the house. It would have been easy enough to learn of Micah's relationship with the two through their business. Both men would be appalled that a computer nerd had managed to tail them without being seen.

His mind worked over everything that had happened. Patsy had said she'd only told Vicki, the store manager, that she was meeting Caylee that day in the park. But, Rick had known as well. He'd said as much to Caylee on the phone. He could have easily hurried to the park before the designated meeting time and waited for Caylee to show up. Dammit, they should have paid more attention to Rick instead of focusing on Patsy.

Caylee's bed squeaked as she shifted positions, obviously finding sleep elusive as well. Micah stared at the window, watching the blinking light, hoping it would hypnotize him into sleep.

Tomorrow was going to be a difficult day, less so for him than for Caylee. The reality of what she suspected would hit her hard.

"Micah? Are you still awake?" Her soft voice floated over to him.

"Yeah."

In the faint illumination of the room he saw her shove the covers off her and get up. In two steps she stood at the side of his bed. She said nothing, but he knew what she wanted, what she needed.

He raised his sheet, and she slid in next to him, her body warm as toast. It never occurred to him not to wrap his arms around her and hold her tight through what remained of the night.

Chapter Eleven

Caylee awoke first, for a moment feeling safe and protected wrapped in Micah's arms. She was curled into him like a piece that fit perfectly into a puzzle. She could tell he was still asleep by his deep, even breathing.

She remained unmoving, reluctant to leave the warmth and security of his sleeping embrace. She squeezed her eyes tightly closed, willing herself to go back to sleep, but her brain was far too awake, working through the horror of the attack she'd survived and the heartbreaking possibility that the cousin she loved like a brother had been responsible.

Why? It was the question that ripped at her guts, tore at her heart. Why would Rick want to kill her? Had he resented her all those years he'd shared his mother with her? Had he hated the motherless child that forced Patsy to divide her time and attention?

If he did resent her, she'd never felt it, never seen

a glimpse of it shining from his dark brown eyes. Had he been that good an actor?

Micah stirred against her, his warm breath on her neck shooting a shiver of pleasure through her. His hand splayed on her stomach and in that simple movement she wanted him.

She took his hand and moved it to her breast as all thoughts of Rick fled her mind. His hand warmed the silk of her nightgown as he caressed her breast through the material.

She felt his arousal against her and turned over in his arms. With her face tucked into the hollow of his throat she smelled his familiar scent…a scent of clean, sleepy male mingling with the faint whisper of his cologne.

They didn't kiss and they didn't speak, but their sleep-warmed bodies moved together slowly at first, then with a building urgency.

His mouth moved down the length of her neck then captured one of her nipples. She gasped with sheer pleasure as he sucked and lavished the turgid tip with his tongue. She stroked down his broad back, loving the feel of muscle beneath warm skin.

She loved this man, whose eyes could frost like winter, but warm her like a summer day. She loved this man who could laugh at himself and tease her with humor. Her love was in her touch and she wanted him to feel it radiating from every fiber of her being.

Within minutes they were both naked, and he'd

put on a condom. She straddled his hips, staring down at him as she took in his hardness.

His hands caressed her breasts as he filled her and she moved against him as heart-pounding sensations rocked through her.

He moved his hands from her breasts to the sides of her hips as she increased her pace, felt the wave of pleasure rising up inside her until she thought she might scream.

She knew the end of their time together was rushing toward them, that they couldn't go on hiding in cheap motels and running from the law much longer. The knowledge only made each touch, each moment of their lovemaking more intense.

All too quickly she would have to tell him goodbye, for even though she was in love with him, he'd never pretended to want anything more from her that what they'd shared.

Faster and faster they moved, their breaths coming in short, quick pants. She felt the press of tears, so immense was her emotional connection with him at the moment.

When her release came, it shuddered through her, melting her bones, and she collapsed on top of him. He gave her only a minute, then rolled her over on her back and stroked into her hard and fast, the cords of his neck taut and his eyes gleaming.

When he reached his release, he spoke for the first time, whispering her name over and over again. She captured the sound of it deep in her heart to warm her. But she knew when this moment passed and she had to face the day ahead, a dreadful cold would creep into her soul.

Afterward they remained in each other's arms. She lay against his chest and listened to the sound of his heartbeat slowing…returning to a more normal beat.

Dawn had come and gone, and the room was now lit with early morning light. She squeezed her eyes closed tightly, as if she could hold back the day.

Despite what they had just shared, she had a bad feeling. She didn't want to face the day. She'd much rather just stay in bed with Micah.

All too soon he stirred and without saying a word he got up, grabbed his clothes and disappeared into the bathroom.

Immediately the icy cold she'd anticipated swept through her, and she shivered and burrowed deeper beneath the sheets. The sound of running water let her know he was in the shower.

It was a new day. And her cousin had tried to kill her. Even though her heart rebelled at the idea, as she thought of those minutes when the person had been on top of her, his hands wrapped around her throat, she knew deep in her heart that it had been Rick.

It wasn't just the scent of spearmint that assured her of the fact, it had been the length of his hair when she'd reached up to grab it, the faint scent of his familiar cologne.

She knew it hadn't been Grant Worthington or somebody Vicki had hired. It hadn't been John Raymond. It had been Rick.

She heard the water shut off, and moments later Micah stepped out of the bathroom. "Why don't I go grab us some breakfast while you shower, then we'll figure out what our next move needs to be."

She wanted it to be getting back into bed and making love again. "Be careful," she said as he headed for the door, aware that anytime either of them were out in public, they ran the risk of arrest.

By nine o'clock Caylee had showered and dressed and Micah was back with their breakfast. They sat on the edge of Cayleee's bed, sipping coffee, eating sausage biscuits and trying to decide what their next move should be.

Micah had called Troy and let him know what had happened and where they were. Troy had promised to dig deeper into Rick's life and see if he could come up with any information that might explain everything.

"I want to look at that list of passengers Troy got us," she said thoughtfully.

"Why? You already looked it over and Rick's name wasn't on any of those lists." Micah finished the last of his biscuit and followed it with the swig of the strong coffee.

She frowned thoughtfully. "While I was showering I was thinking. When Rick was twenty years old, he made himself a fake ID that could have fooled anyone. With his computer skills I imagine he could easily do the same thing today. Now that I know what I'm looking for, I'm sure he's on that list."

Micah got up and opened his duffel bag and retrieved the passenger lists. Caylee set her coffee cup on the nightstand and took them from him. She wanted to believe that she wouldn't find a name remotely like Rick's on the sheets of paper. She still clung to a tiny hope that they were wrong, that she was wrong and it was some crazed stranger who was trying to kill her.

She ran her gaze down the names and that tiny modicum of hope crashed and burned inside her when she spied the name Nick Johnson.

She stabbed a trembling finger on the name, felt the press of new tears aching inside her. "Nick Johnson. Rick Jackson." She looked at Micah. "So close. So easy to change just a letter or two." The papers crumbled in her hand. "It's him, Micah. Rick tried to kill me and I don't know why. I just don't understand why!"

"Maybe Luke and Troy will be able to dig up some answers today. With a specific target to focus on, you'd be amazed what they can find in a short period of time."

"But no matter what they dig up, the information doesn't get us out of this mess unless Chief Kincaid listens to what we find out," she replied.

"You let me take care of Kincaid," he said, his voice hard and determined. "Jackasses are my specialty," he added with a little smile. Although she knew he meant the words to ease her concerns, they didn't.

But the fact that he wanted her to be all right, that he'd tried to make a joke, pushed her love for him to the surface with such force she could no longer keep it inside of her.

"Micah, I told you once that I believe that everything happens for a reason," she began. "I think I know the reason this has happened to us."

He narrowed his eyes slightly, as if already closing himself off to whatever she might have to say. "What?" he asked grudgingly.

"I think it was so we'd find each other," she hurried on, not giving him an opportunity to speak. "I know it sounds crazy, but I've fallen in love with you, Micah. And don't try to tell me that we haven't known each other that long or that I'm deluding myself because of the circumstances we've found ourselves in. I'm thirty years old. Old enough to know what's in my heart and I love you like I've never loved before."

She'd hoped her confession would bring him joy, but instead he stood from the bed and crossed the room, as if needing to distance himself from her and the words she'd just spoken.

"I've told you all along that I like fast women. You aren't a fast woman, Caylee." His eyes were flat as he jammed his hands into his pockets. "I never made any promises to you, never even hinted that there would ever be anything between us. You're a pretty woman. I like you and I find you physically attractive, but I travel light through life."

It was the most he'd ever said since she'd known him, and each and every word broke her heart. She knew she was more to him than just a physically attractive convenience. She knew with a woman's intuition that she meant more to him that he was willing to admit to her or to himself.

"Don't you get lonely, Micah? Traveling light can be very lonely. Don't you want children? A family?"

"I don't need anybody. I like only being responsible for myself. Don't look at me like that, Caylee. I never made any promises."

"I know. You don't make promises." Before she could say anything more his cell phone rang.

He answered and listened for several long minutes as Caylee fought back a new round of tears. Maybe he was right. Maybe there was no reason for anything, and love didn't matter.

After all, she'd thought that Rick loved her. She'd thought he was a piece of her heart, but that hadn't stopped him from trying to kill her.

It was time to end this. She couldn't remain in hiding with Micah and continue to fall deeper and deeper in love with him knowing that love would never be reciprocated.

As Micah finished up his phone call, a plan began to formulate in her head. There was really only one way to end it. If Rick was really guilty, then there was only one way to know for sure.

"Your cousin likes to gamble," Micah said as he clicked off the call.

Caylee frowned. "Rick? A gambler?"

"According to Troy, his personal finances don't show it yet, but he's on the verge of disaster. He's been using his business funds to pay his bills and he's pawned most of his business equipment."

"Pawned his equipment?" She repeated his words, trying to make sense of them. "I knew he enjoyed going to the casinos occasionally here in town, but I had no idea it was a real problem for him."

Micah didn't return to sit next to her on the bed, but instead kept his distance, leaning his slim hip against the dresser. "Initially when Troy checked out Rick, he only did a cursory surface check. This morning he dug deeper and suspects that Rick owes some big money to some mean people. He's desperate, Caylee, and that makes him dangerous."

"But it still doesn't make sense. If I die, he gets nothing. He's not my beneficiary. He's not even in my will."

He frowned thoughtfully. "But Patsy is your beneficiary. And you've said all along that she has never shown an interest in your store. Maybe Rick thinks he can talk his mother into giving the store to him, then he can sell it to the Berkoff Company and dig himself out of the hole that is about to bury him."

For the first time since all this had begun, something finally made sense. It was a horrifying sense, but at least it was an answer. Patsy would do almost anything for her son, just as Caylee had known she'd do almost anything for her.

"So it's all for money," she said with a touch of bitterness. "The funny thing is, if he'd come to me and told me he was in trouble, I would have given him whatever he needed."

"I know." Micah once again jammed his hands into his pockets, a frown creasing his forehead.

She wanted to talk to him about how much she loved him. She wanted to convince him to look deep in his heart because he'd realize he loved her, too. But his eyes held a distance she'd come to recognize that meant he'd closed himself off, wouldn't really hear whatever she tried to say.

It's time to end it. Once again the words reverberated through her head. "I was thinking while you were on the phone," she said. She watched his entire body tense as if he didn't want to hear whatever was one her mind. She drew a deep breath and continued. "I think we need to use me as bait and catch Rick when he tries to kill me again."

"THAT'S A RIDICULOUS idea," Micah instantly scoffed and pulled his hands from his pockets.

He was still reeling with her confession of love for him. He felt off-kilter, irritated by the unusual feeling of loss of control. But, the last thing he wanted to do was put her at risk.

"It's not a ridiculous idea," she protested. "I could have Rick meet me here in this motel room. I could tell him that you and I parted ways, that you left me alone and I don't know where to go or what to do."

She stood, appearing to gain momentum as she continued to speak. "You could hide in the closet or in the bathroom or maybe you and your buddies could wire me and you all could hide in the room next door. I could get Rick to confess to everything and we could get it on tape, then Kincaid would have to believe our story."

Micah shook his head. "It's a bad idea. It's far too dangerous." Her throat still held the evidence of the last attack. He didn't want to take a chance of her being hurt again.

"I can't go on like this, Micah. *We* can't go on like this." Emotion made her voice tremble. "We can't keep running and hiding. Eventually we're going to get caught, and I'd rather end this on my terms. Unless you have a better idea then we should go with mine."

Micah frowned, assessing all the angles of her idea and frantically trying to come up with an alternative of his own. "And what if he bursts through the door and shoots you before you can get a confession, before any of us can get in here to save you?"

"He won't," she replied with an assurance Micah certainly didn't feel. "He won't want to use a gun, not in this place. It might draw attention, and somebody might see him leaving. He won't take that chance." She reached up and touched her neck, still mottled and faintly bruised from the attack the night before.

"He used a gun before," Micah replied and tried to tamp down the rage that rose up inside him as he looked at the discoloration of her throat.

"That was different. We were in a wide, open space and he had a hiding place in the woods. He was confident that nobody would see him there. It doesn't make sense that he'd try to shoot me here. I'm telling you it's the only way to get us out of this, the only way to bring things to a final conclusion."

In his heart he knew she was probably right. Kincaid certainly wasn't listening to him, but he couldn't reject a confession if they could get Rick on tape. But the idea of using Caylee as bait, of putting her at risk, made him feel physically ill.

"Micah, we have to do it. Surely you and your buddies can keep me alive. It's the only plan that makes sense to end this."

"Let me talk to Troy and Luke," he relented. "If they think it's a viable plan then we'll see what we can work out." He picked up his cell phone and headed for the front door. "I'm going to step outside and get some air while I make the calls."

She gazed at him worriedly. "Be careful." She

said that often to him, worried about his safety when it was her life at risk.

He nodded, stepped outside the door and into the midmorning heat. A glance around the parking lot alleviated any fear that somebody might see him. It was as deserted as a cemetery at midnight.

She loved him. He clutched the phone in his hand, not dialing as his mind worked through what she'd said to him. She loved him.

Surely it was only the close proximity that they'd shared over the past week that had her believing that. These were strange circumstances that had brought them together, and what she was feeling had to be manufactured from fear.

It wasn't real. It couldn't be real. He wasn't the kind of man women fell in love with, and he sure wasn't looking for love in his life.

He hadn't lied to her. He'd always traveled light. That's the way he liked it, he told himself firmly. He didn't need anyone.

Had his mother left him behind because she loved him enough to want more for him than she'd ever be able to give him? The thought had never entered his mind until Caylee had mentioned it. For him, her desertion had always been the ultimate betrayal that had guided him through life.

What Caylee had given him was a touch of forgiveness in his heart for the mother who had left him behind, a touch of peace that he'd never known before.

Dammit, she couldn't be in love with him. She was deluding herself. Once this was all behind her and she got back to her real life, he'd be nothing more than a memory of this heartbreaking time in her life.

He punched in Troy's phone number, not wanting to think about love or Caylee another minute. She was right. It was time to get this done, to bring it all to an end.

As he spoke to his partner, he kept his gaze focused on the highway outside the parking lot entrance. If anyone pulled in, he'd step back into the room. He didn't want to take a chance of somebody seeing him, recognizing him from the news stories that had circulated about Jason's death and calling the cops. He'd contact the authorities on his terms.

It was a long conversation as the two men went over the pros and cons of Caylee's plan. Ultimately, they agreed—although Micah with reservations—that it was workable and probably the only course of action they had left.

They agreed to meet at the motel at two that afternoon. The next call Micah made was to Kincaid. As usual he was put right through to the Chief.

"We know who killed Jason Worthington," he said without preamble. "And since then, the same person has made two attempts on Caylee's life. You know about the shooting in the park, but last night somebody tried to strangle her." He quickly told the

Chief of Police about the attack on Caylee the night before and Caylee's belief that it had been her cousin, Rick. He didn't mention the location of the safe house and thankfully Kincaid didn't ask.

"So what do you want from me? I can't do anything about it as long as you two are out there acting like a couple of loose cannons," Wendall replied.

"I have a proposition for you," Micah replied. "We're setting up a sting operation, and we're hoping to get a confession from Rick."

Wendall released a string of curses that would have made a sailor blush. "For God's sakes, let me do my job. Turn yourselves in and let me deal with the investigation end of this mess."

"You haven't heard my proposition yet," Micah exclaimed. "I want you to be here when it goes down, but before I give you any details I need some assurances from you."

There was a long pause. "What kind of assurances?" Kincaid asked grudgingly.

"I don't want Caylee taken in to custody for anything. She's innocent in all of this. I don't want her to spend a minute behind bars. You make it right with her."

There was a long hesitation. "All right. I give you my word as Chief of Police."

"That's not good enough," Micah said. "I need your word as a man." He clenched the phone more tightly against his ear. "You give me your word as a man that Caylee will suffer no consequences in all this, and if Rick isn't guilty you can arrest me."

His words were followed by a stunned silence. It was the biggest gamble of Micah's life. If Caylee was wrong and Rick wasn't responsible for anything that had happened, then Micah would lose everything, including his freedom.

But Caylee was right about one thing. It was time to bring this all to an end. He cared enough about her that he wanted her to be okay. He wanted her to get back to her life and the store that she loved. As long as he could protect her, he'd face whatever he needed to face.

"You really think this cousin of hers is behind it all?" Wendall asked and in that moment Micah knew he'd hooked him.

"Everything points to him, and Caylee believes he was the one who attacked her last night."

"And if you're wrong you'll walk right into my handcuffs?"

"As long as you agree to leave Caylee alone. And if Rick isn't the guilty party, then she's going to need some protection because somebody is trying to kill her." He hesitated a moment, then asked, "Do we have a deal?"

"Why not?" Kincaid replied easily. "You're the one putting everything on the line. I have nothing to lose. My word as a man, Caylee will be viewed as a victim, and if she's in danger we'll do everything possible to keep her safe."

It was all Micah needed to hear. He told Kincaid where they were and exactly what they had planned, then he disconnected.

He drew in a deep breath of the outside air, knowing that if things went wrong it would be the last air he'd breathe as a free man.

Chapter Twelve

Caylee should have felt very well protected with all the men that now occupied the motel room, but as she thought of what was soon to happen, she was as frightened as she'd ever been in her life.

Luke and Troy leaned against one wall in the motel room, their features reflecting the seriousness of the moment. Micah stood nearby, his eyes a cool blue as he watched a police officer named Ron wire Caylee.

Chief Kincaid sat on the edge of the bed. He was a handsome man with dark hair and a smile that didn't quite reach his hazel eyes. The tension between him and Micah had been palpable since Kincaid had arrived at the motel.

Caylee had no idea how Micah had convinced him to be a part of this, but she was grateful that he appeared to be working with them rather than against them.

"We're not only wiring you, we're bugging the room as well," Kincaid said. "Your job is to get your cousin to confess."

"Your job is to stay safe," Micah interjected. "Even if he hasn't confessed, if you sense that you're in danger, you give us a signal and we'll be right here."

She nodded as the police officer stepped away from her. Technology was amazing. The power pack of the wiring unit was no bigger than a small battery. It had been taped to her back. The microphone was an attractive, jeweled flower brooch pinned to her blouse.

As Ron got to work removing the cover switchplate of an outlet, Caylee sank to the edge of the bed opposite Kincaid. Nobody spoke until Ron had a bug planted in the outlet, then Kincaid stood. "We'll test the equipment, then get this thing done and over with." The motel unit next door had been rented for the operation, and that's where the men would hide while Caylee remained here with Rick.

As the men began to file out, Caylee's nerves screamed in her head. What if she was wrong, what if Rick took one step into the room and shot her? What if the equipment malfunctioned and nobody heard her scream for help?

Even though she was the one who had wanted to do this, she was suddenly struck by how many things could go wrong. What if Rick wasn't the guilty party after all? Then all this trouble and worry would be for nothing.

When the men were all gone, she waited a few moments to give them time to get into the room next door. When she thought enough time had passed, she began to pace the room. "Testing. Testing," she said aloud. "I hope you guys can hear me. Am I talking too softly? Do I need to speak up? Maybe this pin needs to be higher on my blouse."

The door to her room opened and Kincaid came back in, followed closely by Micah. "You're coming in loud and clear," Kincaid said. "Just talk normal. You don't want him to think that anything is amiss." He checked the fastening on the pin one last time. "And now it's time to get the guest of honor here."

Caylee's mouth was unaccountably dry as she picked up the cell phone Micah had provided. "You don't have to do this, Caylee," Micah said. "If you're too afraid we can call it all off right now. We'll figure something else out."

She knew if she aborted the plan now, she and Micah would be under arrest. There was no turning back. She forced a smile to her lips. "Let's just get this over with." With a trembling finger she punched in Rick's cell phone number. He answered on the second ring.

"Caylee, we've been wondering when we'd hear from you again. Are you all right?" His familiar voice filled her with a yawning sense of sadness. Was it really possible that he wanted her dead?

"Yes, I mean no, I'm not all right," she replied. She didn't have to pretend to be upset. "Micah and I had a falling out." She looked at the man she loved, and tears blurred her vision because she loved him and he refused to love her back.

She stared down at the ugly bedspread. "He left me, Rick. He left me all alone and now I don't know what to do."

"Where are you, Caylee? I'll come there and we'll figure things out."

"Rick, I'm so scared. I don't know whether to turn myself in or keep on running."

"Just tell me where you are. We'll sort it all out."

She drew a deep breath to steady her racing heart. "I'm at the Lazy Owl Motel near Riverside. Room 108."

"I'll be there in about thirty minutes. Hang tight, Caylee. Everything is going to be all right." He hung up, and Caylee did the same.

"He said he'd be here within thirty minutes," she said to Micah and Kincaid. In thirty minutes she would know if the cousin she'd loved like a brother had betrayed her trust in the most heinous way.

If Rick was the guilty party, then within an hour this would all be over, and Micah would walk out of her life.

Micah shoved his hands in his jean pockets. "It's not too late to change your mind about all this," he said.

She stared at him, trying to read something, anything in his eyes, but it was impossible. He looked as closed off and distant as she'd ever seen him.

Kincaid held out a gun. "You know how to shoot one of these?" he asked.

"Point and pull the trigger?" She'd never touched a gun in her life and didn't even want to think about having to do so now.

Kincaid walked over to the bed and placed the gun under one of the pillows. "Insurance," he said. "Just in case something goes wrong. The safety is off. Don't pull it out unless you intend to use it to save your own life." He moved toward the door. "We'd better get next door in case he shows up early."

"Thank you for being a part of this," she said to him.

He shrugged his broad shoulders. "It's like I told Micah. I have nothing to lose. If Rick Jackson isn't our guilty party, Micah has agreed that I can arrest him instead. With somebody in custody, I'll get the Mayor off my back and that makes me a much happier man."

Caylee shot a startled look at Micah, whose expression didn't change. She looked back at Kincaid. "You mean you're going to arrest both of us if Rick isn't guilty."

Kincaid shook his head. "You'll be free to go. Micah and I made a deal." He turned and left the room as Caylee once again stared at Micah.

"What have you done?" she asked, her voice a mere whisper.

"It needed to end, so I ended it." He pulled his hands out of his pockets and started toward the door. When he reached it, he turned back to her. "By the end of the day you should be back in your own apartment, back in your life where you belong." He didn't wait for her reply, but turned on his heels and left.

Caylee walked over to the door and locked it, then went back to the bed and sat on the edge. Why had he done that? Why had Micah agreed to be arrested in exchange for her going free?

Because he loves you, a little voice whispered in her head. He was giving her back her freedom at the expense of his own. What else could drive a man to do such a thing?

She wanted to run into the room next door and throw herself in his arms. She wanted to tell Kincaid that he had no right to make such a deal, that Micah was as innocent as she was and so should be let go as well.

He loved her and nothing he could say would ever convince her otherwise. Her heart swelled with emotion. And she loved him with every fiber of her being. They belonged together. Fate had brought them together for a reason, and that reason was love.

But before she could claim that love, before she could talk to Micah again, she had to get through the next hour with Rick.

Nerves once again awakened inside her, jangling through her and chilling her heart to arctic temperatures. Her mind filled with all the things that could go wrong. Rick could shoot her dead on first sight. He could grab her around the throat so she couldn't make a sound and the men next door would never know that she was fighting for her life.

Almost as bad was the idea that Rick wasn't guilty, that he'd say nothing to incriminate himself, and Micah would be thrown into jail to await charges of murder.

Although she was certain he would never be convicted due to lack of evidence, the charges against him and the time and energy and money he'd need to fight them would destroy his life.

That possibility was as tragic as her facing the fact that Rick might want her dead. She got up from the bed, too nervous to sit, and began to pace back and forth in the small confines of the room. Her gaze went to the pillow that hid the gun.

Kincaid might as well have tucked a wet noodle beneath the pillow because it would have been as much use as a gun. She couldn't imagine shooting Rick no matter what the circumstances.

Once again she flopped down on the edge of the bed, tears burning at her eyes as she thought of the little boy Rick had been, of the times they'd shared both as children and as adults.

What kind of desperation was he feeling that would have him attempting to commit such a terrible crime? What kind of desperation drove a man to kill a family member? Somebody he loved? She couldn't imagine.

She watched crime shows on television, knew that this kind of thing happened in real life, but had never been able to imagine it happening in her life.

A soft knock on her door had her shooting up off

the bed. Panic seared through her. For a moment she thought she was going to faint. Her heart pounded so fast she was light-headed.

I can't do this. She felt as if her legs might give way. Her entire body trembled. *This is too much, I can't handle it.* She wanted to scream into the wire that this was too hard, that she wanted to call a halt to everything right now.

But a vision of Micah filled her head. Micah, who had gambled his very freedom on what was about to occur. Micah, who was counting on her to get through this so they both could be free.

A strange calm swept over her as the knock sounded again. She could do this for Micah. Legs steadier, and with the dizziness gone, she walked over to the door and cracked it open an inch.

"Caylee?" Rick's deep voice said softly.

"Rick, thank God you came." Her fingers trembled as she unlocked the chain to allow him inside. Her heart began to pound once again as she smelled the familiar scent of him. Spearmint and cheap cologne. It's what she'd smelled the night before when the intruder had tried to strangle her.

"Are you okay?" he asked, his brown eyes radiating concern.

"I am now," she replied and offered him a faint smile.

He motioned toward the bed nearest the door. "Let's sit. We need to figure out what you're going to do."

She was grateful for the solid bed beneath her as

she sat, but uncomfortable as he sat right next to her. "What happened to Stone?" he asked.

"I wanted to turn myself in and he got angry, said we'd spend the rest of our lives in prison. He left and said he wouldn't be back." Tears blurred her vision for a moment. "I didn't know what to do. That's when I thought to call you."

"I'm glad you did. I'll fix things, Caylee. Everything is going to be just fine. I'll fix things for both you and for me." The concern she'd seen in his eyes disappeared beneath a hard, desperate glint.

She thought of the revolver hidden beneath the bed pillow and knew she'd never be able to use it against Rick. As she gazed at him, she saw the little boy she'd taught to ride a bike, the teenager she'd taught to dance.

"What do you mean you'll fix things for both of us? Ricky, what have you done?" she asked softly.

He didn't even pretend not to know what she was asking. He shook his head ruefully. "I got in over my head, Caylee. I've gotten myself in a mess with a gambling problem. I've borrowed money from the wrong people and it's all about to cave in on me."

"Why didn't you come to me? I could have helped you. We could have worked something out," she exclaimed.

"The only way you could have helped me was to give me your store, and I knew that wasn't happening."

She scooted away from him and stared at him

through her veil of tears. "So you tried to kill me in Fortuna?"

"I was beside myself. I couldn't see a way out. I needed your shop, and the only way I could get it was if you were dead." Amazingly he looked at her as if he thought she should understand, like she should accept what he had done.

"You killed Jason."

"A mistake," he replied glibly. "I'm sorry, Caylee, I don't see any other way out." He pulled a knife from his pocket and Caylee jumped up from the bed, momentarily stunned into silence.

"Rick, please."

At that moment the door burst open. Micah was the first one through the door, his expression one of murderous rage. Before he'd gotten both feet inside the room Rick grabbed her, the knife held at her throat.

"Get back," he screamed, the blade of the knife cold and sharp against her skin.

Micah held up his hands. "Okay, all right," he said, his voice deceptively calm, eyes narrowed to mere slits. "We're cool. Just let her go."

"I'll kill her, I swear I will if you don't back out of here," Rick exclaimed. Caylee held her breath, afraid to move a muscle, afraid of the cold steel that caressed her neck.

Micah took two steps backward. "It's over, Rick. If you hurt her, you're just making things worse for yourself." Rick tightened his grip on Caylee, the blade of the knife not moving from her neck.

"Rick, you know how much I love you," Caylee said, her heart pounding like a drum in her head. "Remember when you were eight and we had your birthday party at that place with the clowns, and one of the clowns was mean to you? Remember I went over and smacked him on his big red nose and told him not to be mean to my little cousin ever again."

A strangled cry came from him and Caylee couldn't tell if it was a sob or a laugh. "I taught you to ride your bike," she continued, talking as quickly as possible. "When you were fourteen, I helped you write a love note to Suzie Kendall. I've always been there for you, and if you'd just come to me and told me you were in trouble, we could have figured something out."

This time there was no doubt in her mind that the sound he released was a deep, wrenching sob. He pulled the knife away from her neck and let go of her. She stumbled to the floor as he collapsed on the bed sobbing into his hands.

In mere seconds, Micah had her up and in his arms, and Kincaid had Rick off the bed and in handcuffs. "I'm sorry, Caylee, I'm so sorry," Rick sobbed as Kincaid led him from the motel room and Luke and Troy disappeared as well, leaving the two of them alone.

Caylee hid her face in Micah's broad chest as her

own tears fell freely. There was no question in her mind that Rick would have killed her if Micah hadn't burst into the room. If he'd thought he could get away with it, he would have killed her just to get his hands on the store.

"It's over," Micah said, his hand rubbing down the length of her back. "You did great. We've got his confession on tape. It's finally really over."

She wrapped her arms around his neck and held tight. It might be over for him, but it wasn't over for her. Now that the danger was gone, all threat of arrest was vanished, she was left only with her love for Micah.

She raised her head to look at him, loving the lean angles of his face, the warm glow of his blue eyes as he gazed at her.

He loved her. She knew it in her heart, in her soul. He'd been willing to sacrifice his own personal freedom for her. A man didn't do that for somebody he didn't love.

"Micah, it can't be over," she said. "I'm not ready to tell you goodbye. I love you, and if you look deep into your heart you'll realize that you love me, too."

The warmth of his eyes began to ice over and he dropped his arms from around her. Even without physically distancing himself, she felt him pulling away from her.

"Caylee, we've already had this discussion," he said. He backed away from her and jammed his hands in his pockets, a gesture she'd come to recognize signaled his stress.

"But we didn't have it to the right conclusion," she countered.

"I don't want the same things you do, Caylee. I'm happy with my life just the way it is. Now, get your things together and I'll take you home."

Each word he uttered shattered her heart. She'd been so sure that he loved her, that he'd be willing to take a chance on her…maybe finally have the courage to make a promise, the promise to love her forever.

"You're making a mistake, Micah."

He blinked, but his expression didn't change. "It's my mistake to make," he replied.

She began to gather her items and shove them into the duffel bag, a bitterness rising up inside her. "Maybe I'm a naïve fool after all," she exclaimed. "The cousin I thought loved me as a sister just tried to kill me and the man I believed loved me is choosing to walk away. Maybe love is just a silly notion. I certainly won't make that mistake again."

She gasped as Micah grabbed her by the shoulders. "Stop it," he said, eyes blazing with anger. "Just because I'm damaged goods doesn't mean you have to become the same."

"But you aren't damaged goods," she cried. "You're only that if you choose to be. How much love have you pushed out of your life, Micah? How many of your foster parents might have loved you if you'd just let them? How can you live the rest of your life without letting anyone in? You've shown me you have the capacity to love if you'd just let yourself go."

He dropped his hands to his sides. "I can't."

"Then it really is over," she said and finished gathering her items.

Minutes later they were in the car and he was driving her to her apartment. Neither of them spoke, although this time the silence between them was strained.

For the first time in her life, Caylee was all talked out. There was nothing more for her to say. She couldn't force Micah to love her. All she could do was prepare to pick up the pieces of her own broken heart.

She would mourn Micah just as she would mourn Rick. She wouldn't be the only one devastated by Rick's actions. Aunt Patsy would need her love and support in the days and weeks to come, but at the moment she couldn't focus on her aunt's heartbreak because her own hurt so terribly.

They reached her apartment complex, and she grabbed her duffel bag and jumped out of the car. He started to get out as well, but she stopped him. "No need for long goodbyes," she said briskly. "Thanks for everything, Micah. I hope you have a wonderful life."

Before he could say anything, she turned on her heels and headed for the building. Shoulders back, head held high, she refused to let him see her shed another tear over him. There would be plenty of time for her tears when she got inside her apartment, when she thought of all that might have been.

"I'M GLAD YOU FIRED that snippety young woman," Patsy said as she leaned against the counter that housed the best of the diamonds that Rings and Things carried. "I never did like her."

Caylee smiled at her. "I'll handle things here myself until I find somebody to hire as manager." She'd decided to fire Vicki after everything that had happened. She couldn't trust the young woman knowing she was dating a Berkoff heir and wanted the store as her own.

Caylee now sprayed glass cleaner on the counter-top and swiped it with a clean cloth, her thoughts going back over the past few days.

It had been a week since Rick had been arrested, and Caylee's and Micah's names had finally been cleared, a week of Caylee and Patsy finding strength in each other.

Jason's maid, Marie, had been caught trying to pawn the items that had been stolen on the night of the murder, and Kincaid seemed pleased that all the loose ends had been tied up.

Patsy had known Rick was in trouble, had even pulled money off her credit card in an attempt to help him, but she'd had no idea how deep he was in and how desperate he'd become. As much as she loved her son, she'd been appalled by the lengths he'd been willing to go to in order to help himself. Rick was looking at a long prison term and Patsy had come to grips with it as much as a mother could under the circumstances.

Caylee had tried her best to keep busy over the last week, not wanting to give herself a moment to think about Micah. But, no matter what she was doing, no matter how tired or busy she was, thoughts of him snuck into her mind on a regular basis.

Nighttime was the worst. She thought of those nights she'd spent with him cuddled together on the sofa, talking about nothing important and yet everything that mattered.

They would have been good together. No, they would have been great. She spritzed the counter with more cleaner and rubbed it vigorously.

"Well, dear, I'm going to head on home," Patsy said. She glanced out the window toward the gray skies. "I want to be home before it starts to storm." She waited for Caylee to set down the bottle of cleaner, then the two of them hugged.

"I'm sorry, Caylee," the older woman said for the hundredth time since Rick's arrest.

"There's nothing for you to be sorry about," Caylee exclaimed.

"I didn't raise him to be a horrible man," she said as she worried her hands together.

"He isn't a horrible man, but he did a horrible thing," Caylee replied.

"I just don't understand it," Patsy replied.

Caylee smiled and hugged her once again. "There are some things we'll never understand. Now, go home before the rain starts."

She watched as Patsy walked out into the gray day, then released a deep sigh and went over to her desk. It was going to storm, and she couldn't help but think of Micah as the day darkened.

What was he doing on this stormy day? Was he thinking of her? Had she only imagined that he cared for her? She frowned as a faint roar of thunder sounded in the distance. She didn't want to think about Micah Stone anymore.

Without any customers in the store, she decided to do some bookkeeping. She was absorbed in her work when she heard the tinkle of the bell over the door indicating a customer had arrived.

She looked up and froze as she saw Micah walking toward her. She'd never seen him in anything but jeans and a T-shirt, but today he wore a white shirt and navy dress slacks. He was no less devastatingly handsome in the more formal wear.

Outside the front of her store, she saw Luke and Troy take positions on either side of the door. She stood from her desk, hating how her heart leapt at the sight of him, how her legs felt weak and her stomach jumped with nervous anticipation.

"I see you brought your muscle with you," she said. "If you're here to repossess something you must have the wrong address. All my bills are paid up." She was pleased that her voice sounded cool and collected despite the crazy rush of emotion that swept through her.

"Actually I *am* here to repossess something, but first I want to ask you something. What's your favorite color?"

She frowned at him. "You drove all the way over here to see me with a storm coming to ask me what my favorite color is?"

"Just answer me, Caylee, please."

"I don't know, I've always liked pink a lot, but I like purple, too. Yellow makes me feel happy, you know because it looks like sunshine. Then there's blue, that intense blue of a spring sky…." She broke off, realizing that as usual she was rambling. "Sorry, for some reason I'm feeling very nervous."

"And when you're nervous you talk a lot," he said matter-of-factly.

"What do you want, Micah? Why are you here?" She wanted him to cut to the chase. She couldn't stand looking at him, loving him and not knowing what he wanted from her.

He stuffed his hands in his pockets. "I thought I could do it. I thought I could just walk away from you with no regrets. But I miss you. I miss you taking forever to answer a simple question. I miss the sound of your laughter. I miss that you always see the good in everything, that you saw the good in me."

He pulled his hands from his pockets, his gaze as intense as she'd ever seen. "I need to know if it's too late, if you've changed your mind about the way you feel for me."

She was afraid to grasp the joy that tingled through her, the distinct feeling that something wonderful was about to happen. "As you've reminded me before, I'm not a fast woman, Micah. When I love, I love deep and hard, and nothing has changed about the way I feel for you."

He took two steps toward her and she met him halfway, melting into the arms that she had missed, the arms of the man she loved.

"Caylee, I love you," he said. "I love you like I've never loved another person. I want to build a life with you." Her heart sang at the sound of the words she'd most wanted to hear from him. "I promise you, Caylee, that we're going to have a wonderful life together."

"But you said you came here to repossess something," she said.

"My heart." He smiled. "When you left you took my heart. But I've decided you can keep it." He raised a hand and touched her cheek in a soft caress. "Now tell me, do you believe in a long engagement or a short one?"

Her heart swelled inside her. "Right now, with your arms around me, I think a short engagement would be nice. But, there are positives about a long engagement. It would give me time to pull together a wonderful wedding. But then again, who cares about a wonderful wedding. The most important thing is that we're together."

"Caylee?"

"Yes?"

"Shut up and kiss me."

She laughed and raised her lips to meet his and they shared a kiss that promised a lifetime of love and a beautiful future. When the kiss ended, a clap of thunder sounded overhead.

"It's going to storm," she said.

The smile he offered her was like a burst of sunshine, warming her heart in all the right places. "I think finally the storms in my life are over."

He hugged her, and as he did, she glanced over his shoulder and saw that it had begun to rain. "Your friends are getting wet," she said.

He grinned again. "They're ex-Navy SEALS. They know how to weather a storm." He lowered his lips to hers again and she knew she was where she belonged.

* * * * *

*In honor of our 60th anniversary, Harlequin®
American Romance® is celebrating by featuring an
all-American male each month, all year long with*
MEN MADE IN AMERICA!
*This June, we'll be featuring American men
living in the West.*

Here's a sneak preview of
THE CHIEF RANGER by Rebecca Winters.

*Chief Ranger Vance Rossiter has to confront the
sister of a man who died while under Vance's
watch…and also confront his attraction to her.*

"Chief Ranger Rossiter?" The sight of the woman who'd stepped inside Vance's office brought him to his feet. "I'm Rachel Darrow. Your secretary said I should come right in."

"Please," he said, walking around his desk to shake her hand. At a glance he estimated she was in her midtwenties. Her feminine curves did wonders for the pale blue T-shirt and jeans she was wearing. "Ranger Jarvis informed me there's a young boy with you."

The unfriendly expression in her beautiful green eyes caught him off guard. "Yes," was her clipped reply. "When we arrived in Yosemite the ranger told me I couldn't go anywhere in the park until I talked to you first."

"That's right."

"Knowing you wanted this meeting to be private, he offered to show my nephew around Headquarters."

So this woman was the victim's sister…. "What's his name?"

"Nicky."

The boy who haunted Vance's dreams now had a name. "How old is he?"

"He turned six three weeks ago. Were you the man in charge when my brother and sister-in-law were killed?"

"Yes. To tell you I'm sorry for what happened couldn't begin to convey my feelings."

The woman's gaze didn't flicker. "I won't even try to describe mine. Just tell me one thing. Was their accident preventable?"

"Yes," he answered without hesitation.

"In other words, the people working under you fell asleep on your watch and two lives were snuffed out as a result."

Hearing it put like that, he had to set the record straight. "My staff had nothing to do with it. I, myself, could have prevented the loss of life."

Ms. Darrow's expression hardened. "So you admit culpability."

"Yes. I take full blame."

A look of pain crossed over her features. "You can just stand there and admit it?" Her cry echoed that of his own tortured soul.

"Yes." He sucked in his breath.

"I work for a cruise line. Aboard ship, it's the captain's responsibility to maintain rigid safety regulations. If a disaster like that had happened while he was in charge he would have been relieved of his command and never given another ship again."

Rachel Darrow couldn't know she was preaching to the converted. "If you've come to the park with the intention of bringing a lawsuit against me for negligence, maybe you should." It would only be what he deserved.

"Maybe I will."

In the next instant, she wheeled around and hurried out of his office. Vance could have gone after her, but it would cause a scene, something he was loath to do for a variety of reasons. In the first place, he needed to cool down before he approached her again.

The discovery of the Darrows' frozen bodies had affected every ranger in the park. A little boy had been orphaned—a boy whose aunt was all he had left.

* * * * *

Will Rachel allow Vance to explain—and will she let him into her heart?
Find out in
THE CHIEF RANGER
Available June 2009 from
Harlequin® American Romance®.

We'll be spotlighting a different series every month
throughout 2009 to celebrate our 60th anniversary.

Look for Harlequin®
American Romance® in June!

Join us for a year-long celebration of the rugged
American male! From cops to cowboys—
Men Made in America has the hero
you've been dreaming about!

Look for

The Chief Ranger

by Rebecca Winters, on sale in June!

Bachelor CEO by Michele Dunaway	July
The Rodeo Rider by Roxann Delaney	August
Doctor Daddy by Jacqueline Diamond	September

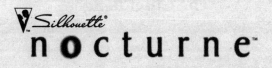

REQUEST YOUR FREE BOOKS!

2 FREE NOVELS PLUS 2 FREE GIFTS!

HARLEQUIN®

INTRIGUE®

Breathtaking Romantic Suspense

YES! Please send me 2 FREE Harlequin Intrigue® novels and my 2 FREE gifts (gifts are worth about $10). After receiving them, if I don't wish to receive any more books, I can return the shipping statement marked "cancel." If I don't cancel, I will receive 6 brand-new novels every month and be billed just $4.24 per book in the U.S. or $4.99 per book in Canada. That's a savings of close to 15% off the cover price! It's quite a bargain! Shipping and handling is just 50¢ per book.* I understand that accepting the 2 free books and gifts places me under no obligation to buy anything. I can always return a shipment and cancel at any time. Even if I never buy another book from Harlequin, the two free books and gifts are mine to keep forever.

182 HDN EYTR 382 HDN EYT3

Name	(PLEASE PRINT)

Address	Apt. #

City	State/Prov.	Zip/Postal Code

Signature (if under 18, a parent or guardian must sign)

Mail to the Harlequin Reader Service:
IN U.S.A.: P.O. Box 1867, Buffalo, NY 14240-1867
IN CANADA: P.O. Box 609, Fort Erie, Ontario L2A 5X3

Not valid to current subscribers of Harlequin Intrigue books.

**Are you a current subscriber of Harlequin Intrigue books and want to receive the larger-print edition?
Call 1-800-873-8635 today!**

* Terms and prices subject to change without notice. Prices do not include applicable taxes. Sales tax applicable in N.Y. Canadian residents will be charged applicable provincial taxes and GST. Offer not valid in Quebec. This offer is limited to one order per household. All orders subject to approval. Credit or debit balances in a customer's account(s) may be offset by any other outstanding balance owed by or to the customer. Please allow 4 to 6 weeks for delivery. Offer available while quantities last.

Your Privacy: Harlequin is committed to protecting your privacy. Our Privacy Policy is available online at www.eHarlequin.com or upon request from the Reader Service. From time to time we make our lists of customers available to reputable third parties who may have a product or service of interest to you. If you would prefer we not share your name and address, please check here. ☐

HI09R

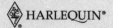
HARLEQUIN®

INTRIGUE®

COMING NEXT MONTH

Available June 9, 2009

#1137 BIG SKY DYNASTY by B.J. Daniels
Whitehorse, Montana: The Corbetts
The hunky ranch owner believes his deranged ex-wife is dead—until he finds out she has returned to town and wormed her way into the life of a sweet and trusting knit shop owner. He's ready to risk his life to save them both from a dangerous obsession.

#1138 PULLING THE TRIGGER by Julie Miller
Kenner County Crime Unit
A suspected murderer has escaped into the mountains, but two of Kenner County's finest are hot on his trail. The only thing hotter is the attraction that still sizzles between these former lovers. Can they catch their man and resurrect their love?

#1139 MIDNIGHT INVESTIGATION by Sheryl Lynn
The feisty skeptic is unimpressed by the tall, well-built police officer who claims psychic abilities—until she unknowingly invites a malevolent spirit home. Now the man she doubted may be the only one who can help....

#1140 HEIRESS RECON by Carla Cassidy
The Recovery Men
The former-navy SEAL is in the business of recovery, but he never figured his job would call for repossessing a beautiful heiress. He has promised her father that he will keep her safe from the threats that are being made against her life, but can he guard his heart as well?

#1141 THE PHANTOM OF BLACK'S COVE by Jan Hambright
He's a Mystery
The isolated clinic in Black's Cove holds many secrets, and the investigative journalist is ready to uncover all—until the owner's grandson tries to stop her. Can these secrets be dangerous enough to endanger both of their lives?

#1142 ROYAL PROTOCOL by Dana Marton
Defending the Crown
When the opera house he designed is overtaken by rebels, the prince stays behind to protect his masterpiece—and the beautiful young diva that is trapped with him. Surviving opening night takes on a whole new meaning as they fight for their lives.

HICNMBPA0509